HOME *is the* HUNTER

Home
is the
Hunter

And Other Stories by
Meg Files

John Daniel & Company
P U B L I S H E R S
Santa Barbara ★ *1996*

Copyright ©1996 by Meg Files
All rights reserved
Printed in the United States of America

"The Mill Pond" first appeared in *Valley Guide Quarterly;* "The Living Desert," "The Night of the Child," "Safeway," and "The Pressure to Modulate" first appeared in *Buffalo Spree Magazine;* "Little Egypt" first appeared in *Inside, Outside* (Snake Nation Press anthology); "Comparative Demographics of A.M. & P.M. Transit Riders" first appeared in *Ellipsis;* "Serpentine" first appeared in *Chiron Review;* "High Country" and "The Kiss" first appeared in *Tucson Guide Quarterly;* "Home is the Hunter" first appeared in *Playgirl.*

Design and typography by Jim Cook

Published by John Daniel & Co., Publishers, a division of Daniel & Daniel, Publishers, Inc., Post Office Box 21922, Santa Barbara, California 93121

LIBRARY OF CONGRESS CATALOGING-IN-PUBLICATION DATA
Files, Meg
    Home is the hunter: and other stories / Meg Files.
    p. cm.
    ISBN 1-880284-14-6 (pbk: alk. paper)
    I. Title.
PS3556.I426H66   1996
813'.54—dc20   95-13873
                                                          CIP

Contents

The Mill Pond / 9

The Living Desert / 22

The Night of the Child / 36

Safeway / 44

The Pressure to Modulate / 49

The Blood and the Blood and the Blood / 60

High Country / 67

Little Egypt / 79

The Kiss / 89

Comparative Demographics of A.M. & P.M. Transit Riders / 93

Serpentine / 105

Home is the Hunter / 116

For my father

To Henry & family,
Presented by Harold S. Bryan,
father of the author.
October 1996

The Mill Pond

BEFORE the accident, the paper mill pond had been like quicksand: mysterious swallower, lovely terror. Even from the big white house on Cedar Street, even across the traffic of Oriole, the mill pond sucked at Frankie. And she did not fight the suction. Flailing in quicksand, she knew from books, only drowned the victim all the faster. The way to survive quicksand was to float.

She'd go two blocks down Oriole to cross at the light, not because it was safer but only because it was away from her mother's view. Magnolia, the street that turned toward the pond, was paved for a block, and the houses were small, wooden, painted blue and lavender and yellow, and the little yards were crowded with cars on blocks and rusty tricycles; the next block was tarmac and trailers. Then the road was overgrown dirt. From here she turned at the cairn of treadless tires onto the path. The weeds were dense and limp. Beneath the willows were secret bare rings of dirt.

She had never really seen the mill pond because the cattails were so thick and tall, much taller than she. She only knew that the pond was huge, occupying all the blocks between Magnolia and Ash to the north. Later, after the accident, she wished that she could fly above and see the span and the shape of the pond. Near the water, the ground was soft, and then it became sludgy: ripe black sludge crusted with gray.

At first, she went to the pond by herself, and once she was in the weeds, she tried to lose herself. Every summer, when the family went to visit Grammy and Grampa Buchwalter in Bucks County, Pennsylvania, she and her sister Lucy would walk into the cornfield, marching right and left, zigzagging until they were lost.

"We're making a parallelogram," Frankie had told her sister, not because she really saw their pattern in the corn but because she loved to say the sixth-grade word.

On the way to the cattails, she would leave the path and weave through the high weeds, trying to lose herself. To the north, the sky was chalky from the paper mill's smokestacks. She could zigzag among the weeds and dip under a willow to eat her peanut butter-and-banana sandwich, but then if she headed toward the white sky, she'd start to sink with each step into the wet dirt, and soon her saddle shoes would be polished with silt and sludge, and she'd reach the cattails, not lost at all.

On the way home, as soon as she hit the tarmac, she walked in her popcorn bobby socks, beating her shoes together. She shook like their flea-powdered black spaniel to get rid of the gray dust.

"Where've you been?" her mother said. "Looks like you've been up somebody's flue."

"Oh, just Lily's basement," she said. Lily Marshall's father was building a bomb shelter in the basement. "Want me to throw down your slippers?" she said and ran upstairs in the big white house. She hated it when her mother asked her to go upstairs and throw down the slippers.

Once when she was supposed to stay home with Lucy while their parents went to an after-school civil defense meeting at the elementary school—Lucy's school, for Frankie was at the middle school—she took her sister to the paper mill pond. Their father had even left work to go to the meeting.

"You two mind your p's and q's," their mother said. She was dressed up in a wool skirt and tall shoes.

Frankie hadn't even gone down to the light but pulled Lucy across Oriole when the traffic broke. Lucy had her eight-inch dolls, Cubby and Karen, along, and she put them under her sweater as soon as the chalky dust rose from the weeds and settled on them.

"Cubby and Karen want to go home," Lucy said.

"No they don't," Frankie said. "Wait till they see the cattails. They'll like the cattails."

"We're getting dirty," Lucy said.

"No, we're not," Frankie said grandly. "We're getting alabaster."

The Mill Pond

But before they got to the cattails, Lucy dropped Cubby and began to cry. "I'm sinking," she said, flailing her arms.

"Don't be a baby," Frankie said, sinking too in the loam.

"It stinks," Lucy cried.

Frankie led her sister back to the path and out past the cairn of tires. She'd never smelled the stink before. At home she made Lucy change into her playclothes. They bathed Cubby and Karen and put them in their matching bathrobes.

"Please don't tell," Frankie said, as shamed as if she'd made Lucy go potty under the willow.

For a month, she took Lily Marshall to the pond. They loaded scrap wood and bent nails from Lily's basement into her little brother Jefferson's wagon, towed it to the Cedar Street house, and added a dozen half-rotted fence planks that Frankie's dad had stacked behind the garage.

"What good's *wood for* a bomb shelter, anyway?" Frankie said.

They crossed at the light, two big girls with a child's wagon.

Lily shrugged. "He's fixing up the inside," she said. "With paneling or something."

Near the cattails, they pulled weeds until they had a clearing. Frankie took off her shoes and socks. Her feet sank in the muck, and when she pulled her feet out, they were black and silty, as if they were coated with fish eggs, and the ankles were trimmed in chalky gray.

"Ick, I'm keeping my shoes on," Lily said.

"My mom'd have a cow if I got these shoes all mucky," Frankie said.

"My mom won't even notice," Lily said.

With Lily's father's hammer, they pounded the fence planks onto two cross boards to make a raft. They worked on Saturdays, and on the third Saturday they dragged the heavy raft from the sludge to the pond's edge.

"If they bomb us," Frankie said, "can I get in your bomb shelter with you?"

"They won't," Lily said. "My mom says."

"Yeah but if they do," Frankie said.

"Yeahbit yeahbit," Lily said. "My mom said he's a paranoid wastrel." She said it proudly.

They dragged the raft through the cattails, bending several underneath. They waded into the water to their knees, and then they hopped onto the crooked, beautiful raft. Lily lost one saddle shoe in the clay. Immediately the raft sank beneath them in the thick brown-gray water.

"Oh no," Frankie said. "Why didn't it work?" She stood in the water, her submerged feet on the fence planks. She had pictured them poling and then paddling all over the pond. She had believed that they'd reach the middle of the pond and float in the circle of cattails that hid the corrugated sludge, and that the white sun would turn the water silver like mercury.

"Get my shoe," Lily said.

And Frankie squished around the sunken raft, but she didn't step on the lost shoe.

"Crap," Lily said. "How am I supposed to walk home?"

"You could hop," Frankie said, choking, trying not to laugh.

"My dad says we can't have anybody else in the shelter," Lily said. "Just him and Mom and Jefferson and me. There's no more air or water or anything. My dad says the rest of the world can go kiss itself."

After that, Frankie went to the pond by herself. She wandered west, following the cattails, farther than she'd ever been, then turned north toward the white sky above the mill itself. The cattails made a ninety-degree turn, and Frankie thought that the pond must be square, industrial, unnatural.

Close enough for her to see the gray, heavy shape of the mill, the ground became too marshy to continue. And she was relieved, watching the dreadful smokestacks, lurching as the mud sucked, held, and released her feet, that she couldn't reach the mill.

She reached up and stroked and shook a cattail until the silk beneath the brown fuzz was loosened. The white silk floated across the pond.

When she found just the right willow, she made herself a shelter within the magic circle of leaves. Among the trash at the edge of the dirt road, she found an old yellow shower curtain, which she folded moldy side in, and an orange crate. Under the willow, on the shower curtain's dry ground, beneath the crate, she hid last winter's snow boots, a jar of M&Ms, and a cardboard-cover book.

She wore the boots to the pond's edge until the leather was muck-stained and circled with levels of white crust, like the high-tide salt-scum lines on the pilings she'd seen when her grandparents took her to Asbury Park. Raspberry Park, her father always called it. After school, she'd walk to the cattails, and then she'd backtrack to her willow and read. At last she'd wear her clean shoes home and set the table and pass the rolls to her father, who always ate for the hunger that cometh, and she'd dry the dishes and do her homework and bathe off the shimmer of secret dust.

"You're kind of quiet these days," her mother said.

Frankie shrugged.

"You're starting to develop," her mother said. "That's good. I was flat as a board when I married your father."

Frankie shrugged in her flannel nightgown.

"Is there anything bothering my big girl?" her mother said. "It might help to get it out of your system."

Frankie shook her head, and was glad that her mother did not see the quick tears that hit the flannel and were absorbed. Nothing could be said about the scary, special suction of the pond, about the circles of white crust rising on her hidden snow boots, about the way her little sister Lucy looked at her and then turned away to move her eight-inch dolls to other rooms in the big dollhouse, about the swelling rubbing against the rough cotton undershirt, about the soft pain as her father patted her mother's bottom when she was helpless with her hands in the dishwater, about the secret walls of shelters.

When Frankie was fifteen, her mother lost a baby.

"Doesn't that sound weird?" she asked her best friend, Kate. They were walking to the A&W down Oriole. "How in the hell do you lose a baby you've never had? Or like you just can't find it but it'll show up eventually in the basement or something."

"But aren't you sad?" Kate said.

It was early spring, Frankie and Kate both wore white pleated skirts, and nobody believed in the bomb any more, not really. Frankie hadn't been to the paper mill pond in two years.

"She didn't even tell us she was, you know," Frankie said.

"Pregnant," Kate whispered.

"My sister's the one who's all worked up. You'd think somebody murdered her best friend or something. Not that she has any best friends to be murdered. But you know."

At the A&W, they ordered the large mugs and chili dogs.

"I mean, Lucy just starts her, you know, and then Mom loses the baby," Frankie said. "My sister is a mess these days."

"I feel sorry for her," Kate said.

"Well, me too," Frankie said. "But you go live with her."

She never told Kate, not even Kate, about her parents down in the basement fighting, about finding Lucy sitting on the toilet lid upstairs with the laundry chute door open. In the basement, their mother wailed and their father's voice was low. Lucy was crying, and Frankie tried to pull her out of the bathroom.

"It's okay," she said. "You don't have to cry."

Their father yelled, "Goddamn it, Betty," and their father never yelled, and they could hear their mother yelling something and crying.

"Okay, okay," Frankie said. "But it'll *be* okay. She just needs to get it out of her system. That's all. Don't you get all worked up too."

Suddenly Frankie despised the onions on the chili dog and the way the root beer made her burp.

"I can't eat this crap," she said.

"Well, give it to me," Kate said. "Give to the poor." Her voice warbled pitifully.

Suddenly Frankie couldn't take Kate either, the way she tried so damn hard. She slid off her stool.

"Hey, did you hear Helen O'Hara sat on chocolate?" Kate said, trying to hold her with gossip. Every time some girl started her period unprepared, she passed the stain off as chocolate.

"Why the hell do we all wear these stupid white skirts anyway?" Frankie said, heading for the door. "I gotta go."

"Fifth hour. Mr. Radebaugh," Kate said desperately. "Call me tonight," she called.

On Saturday, June 23, two weeks before Frankie's sixteenth birthday, her parents drove her and Lucy to the Hoogendykes' house on Ash Street, just north of the paper mill. Frankie was hired at fifty cents an hour to baby-sit for Georgie and Henry Hoogendyke while the four parents went to a Summer Solstice party. Frankie's mother wore a diaphanous gown that she'd made herself. Lucy was along because she was scared to stay alone in the Cedar Street house, though their mother said it was so Lucy could learn some baby-sitting skills and take on some jobs of her own one of these days.

"Oh Betty," Jan Hoogendyke said, "trust you to come up with the original outfit. I love it." She looked down at her own shirtwaist.

"So do I," Hal Hoogendyke said. "You really going to let her out in that, Frank?"

Her mother turned in slow motion, and the fan on the floor caught the material and blew it against her body.

"It's called sea foam green," she said.

"Don't you let those boys run you ragged, Frances," Mrs. Hoogendyke said.

After they left in the Buchwalters' Falcon, Frankie got Georgie and Henry into their sleepers and gave them Neapolitan ice cream and read from their Little Golden Books. They were cute kids, she thought, and that was lucky, with names like George and Henry Hoogendyke. Lucy ate the strawberry ice cream stripes that the boys didn't like.

"It's icky-yucky," Georgie said.

"It's pinky-pukey," Henry said.

When the boys were in bed, Frankie did up the sinkful of dishes, which she knew would ensure another job at the Hoogendykes', while Lucy looked in cupboards until Frankie made her quit. They were asleep on the couch and in the recliner when the parents returned.

The hem of her mother's sea-foam green dress was all wet, and her mother looked wilted. She hiccuped.

"For God's sake, Betty, don't be a cliché," her father said.

"For Bacchus' sake," her mother said. She hiccuped. "Anyway, it isn't as if you tipped nary a glass yourself."

"Go home, you two," Mr. Hoogendyke said. "Gather up your fair young maidens here and take ye all home."

"Isn't this embarrassing?" Mrs. Hoogendyke asked Frankie. "A little summer solstice wine and they go poetic on us."

"And bourbon," Mr. Hoogendyke said.

Their father saw Frankie and Lucy into the Falcon's back seat and their mother into the passenger's seat. Then he disappeared around the side of the Hoogendykes' garage.

"What's Daddy doing?" Lucy said.

"Don't ask," their mother said.

Frankie watched him return, zipping up, stumbling on the lawn.

"Daddy, you peed in their yard!" Lucy said.

"You can't fault a man for doing God's work," he said.

He backed the blue Falcon up, shifted and missed drive, and tried again. They weaved their way down Ash Street.

"Did you two have fun?" Frankie said. Her best friend Kate said you were supposed to engage a drunk in conversation or he could pass out.

"I believe your dear mother might have had some fun," he said carefully. "Some fun in the back yard." He was leaning forward with his chest on the wheel, watching the road. The streetlights made the road look pink-orange.

"Oh Frank, everybody was kissing everybody," her mother said.

"Daddy!" Lucy said urgently.

A black van was charging down the middle of Ash Street, and they were in the middle of Ash Street, and as it neared Frankie saw the orange light from the streetlamps strike the van's black shine and bounce like beads.

"For God's sake, Frank," her mother said.

He turned the wheel and turned the wheel and the Falcon slewed as if the road were wet. The black van smacked them on Lucy's and their mother's side and they spun, Frankie's head held to the back of the seat, and from the rear the van hit them again, so hard it seemed silent, ramming her and Lucy against the front seat, and the car flew straight into the mill pond, skimming across the water as if it were on skis.

Then they stopped, and in the pause Lucy cried, "Ow, Daddy, ow, my legs are cut off." The car sank slowly. The headlights shone beneath the water. Frankie thought her legs must be cut off too. The lighted water was white, thick and white, and the sky was black smeared with chalk. She saw pink spit drooling from Lucy's mouth, and then all the lights disappeared.

"All right, all right now," their father said, "let's take stock here."

The Mill Pond

Their mother turned, saying, "Girls?" and the car sank in the water.

"It'll stop," Frankie said. "It'll hit bottom in a minute." Even though she believed she had no legs, she could feel the fence-post raft dropping in the sludge.

"Nobody move," their father said.

Lucy fell against her, though, and the water ran through the windows.

"Damn it, roll up the windows," he said, but Lucy had fainted and Frankie's legs were gone, and they were sitting in the water. She remembered the old gray smell of the water, just as if she were thirteen again, alone among the cattails.

Their father turned and felt their legs. "Come on, sweetheart," he said, "pull your legs up, and we'll get little Lucy up, and we'll all just swim out of here. Come on now."

"No," Frankie said, numb in the black white water. The water touched her breasts. "Our legs are cut off."

He pulled on her thigh, and she felt nothing but the tug on her dead leg. The water rose to her neck and into her mouth, and she choked. He yanked her thigh, and she screamed and sucked in the foul water and choked.

Their mother knelt on the front seat and held Lucy's head above the water.

"The seat," their mother yelled. "They're jammed under the seat."

"No screaming," their father said. "Frankie, pull your chin up. Do your legs hurt?"

And they didn't hurt. They might not be cut off, she thought, but it didn't matter.

"I can't get out," she said. "It doesn't matter. Go on, you swim away. I know how to do it."

She tipped her face to the ceiling. She thought she could see the rows of holes in the upholstery like black stars in the white sky.

"Oh Frank," she heard her mother say, and Frankie held her breath to turn forward toward her parents with her mouth and nose in the water.

"Float," she tried to say, choking.

In the white white dark Frankie saw her mother and her father look at each other in the front seat. She nodded and he nodded.

"We love you, girls," their mother said. "Frankie. Lucy."

The water touched Frankie's upturned chin. "I don't—" she said.

"Shh, shh," their father said. "I know you don't. Let's all just take it easy."

Frankie held her breath. This pond water could not hurt her, she thought. Or maybe she'd been wrong, hiding at this secret dirty place, and now it had caught her. Sheets of beaded blackness shimmered over her. She could not float.

When Frankie was a senior, Brent Eastwood pushed her down on the back seat of his Camaro.

"Don't you mess with me like that," she said. "You let me up."

"You gave me the come-on," he said. "Don't you tease me, Frances Buchwalter."

She struggled upright. She'd been kissing him, and maybe that was teasing.

"All right, I'm going to tell you about another time in a back seat," she said.

"I don't want to hear it," Brent said. "I've heard about you already."

"So you tried to push me down on the back seat," she said. "You've heard about me."

She'd almost told him, stupid Brent Eastwood. Yes, she'd been wild. Her old best friend Kate had been born again six months after the accident and had burned all their naughty notes to each other. But all that was Kate's imagination, Frankie thought. You didn't need Jesus to die for you when he'd already been dead a zillion years before you were even born and when you had somebody else to die for you anyway. She'd told Kate about the rescue, the truck on treads and the giant magnet that pulled the Falcon from the mill swamp, the ambulances and the oxygen, but she hadn't told Kate about the secret look between her parents who could have climbed through the windows and floated away.

"Get the hell away from me," she told Brent. "You'd never in a zillion years understand."

The Mill Pond

Frankie had turned wild, secure and daring—how dare they agree to die for her?—but Lucy, never having seen her parents look at each other in the luminescent dark, had retreated like a scared guppy to its tiny mossy castle.

When they were in the hospital sharing a room, Frankie had said, "You know Mom and Dad were going to go down with us."

But Lucy had covered her ears. "I can't hear you," she'd chanted. "I can't hear anything in the world."

In the Camaro's back seat, Frankie said, "Home, James. I mean Brent." She laughed.

He slammed the door and got behind the wheel. "You're a cock . . . a tease, Frances. I'm going to tell everyone, all the guys."

"You can say it," Frankie said. "Cock-tease. I've heard it before. And you know what? I don't care who in the world you tell anything."

Once you've sunk below the water and drowned, she thought grandly, nothing can touch you.

For their parents' fortieth anniversary, Frankie and Lucy went back to the big white house on Cedar Street. Frankie and Matt unpacked in her old blue-and-white bedroom, and the kids unrolled their sleeping bags in the basement.

"I kind of feel sorry for old Lucy," Frankie said, "there in her old bed all alone."

"So invite her in," Matt said. "It's not a big bed, but there's such a thing as charity."

"This wealth we don't share," Frankie said. "It's mine, mine, mine." She leapt at him and they fell to the bed.

"Frankie!" her mother called up the stairs. "How about helping me with the decorations?"

"Subtle, Mother," Frankie said to Matt. "Very subtle."

At the party, only Jan Hoogendyke mentioned the ancient accident. "I'll never forget that night," she told Frankie. "It was us who heard it and called for help. Did you ever know that? Thank God you all made it. Thank God you all recovered."

"Right," Frankie said. "So how come you never had me babysit for Georgie and Henry again?"

For years Frankie had felt the silver scum of the pond coating her skin, but Mrs. Hoogendyke must have imagined her lurching out of the sludge stiff-limbed and wicked.

"Lucy!" Frankie called. "Come over here and talk to Mrs. Hoogendyke. Remember her?"

"Of course!" Lucy said. "We baby-sat for you that awful night." She laughed. "So how are those boys, I forget their names?"

"Georgie has a baby and a half," Mrs. Hoogendyke said. "He and Shirley are coming home this Christmas. "Let me show you—"

While she fumbled in her purse, Frankie checked out her own sweet imperfect children across the room.

"Frankie, I want to tell you something," Lucy said, low.

"Here!" Mrs. Hoogendyke flashed a Polaroid of a stiff, fat baby in red sleepers.

"Adorable," Frankie said.

"Frankie," Lucy said, pulling her toward the kitchen.

"Henry's in law school!" Mrs. Hoogendyke called.

Matt patted her fanny as she went by. "More champagne?" he said.

"Lord, no," Frankie said. "How about my little sis?"

But Lucy was already in the kitchen.

"Lucy, what's wrong?" Frankie said.

"Oh nothing, nothing," her sister said. "Things are good. You know I've been in therapy. I know you won't laugh. My inner child has been born!"

"Oh my dear," Frankie said.

"Don't tell Mom and Dad," Lucy said. "They won't get it."

They moved down the counter as the blue crowd moved toward the ice bucket, the men in light blue slacks, the women in sequined sweaters that reflected all blues.

"Last year I made this tape," Lucy said. "My therapist suggested it. I turned off the lights in my apartment. I tried to talk to them but I only cried. Cried for a good half hour. Cried and cried and cried."

"Well, what about?" Frankie said.

"Oh, everything," Lucy said. "How they treated me. How fucked up I was."

"We had the same parents," Frankie said. They moved down to the washer-and-dryer set, away from the party.

"No, we didn't," Lucy said darkly.

"Well, I was older," Frankie said. And I was conscious when the car sank, she thought, and I saw the look they shared.

"Anyway, I brought the tape home and I made them listen to it. They sat in the living room across from each other, Dad in his recliner, and I sat on the floor beside the tape player. The tape wailed for twenty minutes and they kept patting the dog and trying to get up."

Frankie laughed.

"Daddy kept saying, 'Look at poor Kishy, she can't figure out where it's coming from.' And I'm just howling and sobbing away on the tape." She was laughing, too.

After the party, Frankie bedded the kids down in the basement, loaded the dishwasher, and hugged her parents on the way upstairs to her husband.

"I had too much champagne," she said. "But I want to say. We never talked about it. But now—"

"But now your father and I are going to bed," her mother said. "Some things, there's nothing to say."

Upstairs her sister gestured to her. In her yellow childhood bedroom, Lucy took out a cloth doll with a dimpled plastic face. The doll wore a pink pinafore.

"I had to buy it," Lucy said. "Say it's silly, go ahead."

"What's it for?" Frankie said.

"It's my inner child!" Lucy said.

"How could I be so slow?" Frankie said.

"I mean it symbolizes," Lucy said.

"They always loved you, you know," Frankie said. "More than you know."

Lucy wept and Frankie tucked her under the green and yellow quilt their Grammy Buchwalter had made.

In her room, Matt was asleep. Beside him under the blue and white quilt, she stared at the stippled white ceiling. She remembered shaking a cattail until the silk loosened and floated on the water. They wouldn't have died for her and Lucy but with them. All her life her skin would wear the white dust of the evaporated water.

The Living Desert

SHE was not stupid. But she had forgotten that people had pasts. Her life was her own making, and when Nicky Feldman moved on, the California coast's green water disappeared, the glistening kelp and all the limpets and periwinkles in the tidepools vanished. Then in Arizona the green-barked trees, whose name she didn't yet know, sprang to existence, and the four ranges of mountains surrounding the city appeared and the city itself materialized.

Before Nicky could learn the factions, which secretaries were favored by which faculty members, who was on whose side against whom, the art teacher sat on her desk and said, "So you're from California. Bring any good weed?"

He had a thick half-moon mustache that should have carried the corners of his mouth down; instead, his lips kept smiling while the mustache frowned. Nicky did not examine his eyes for the truth.

"I'm here now," she said. "I'm not *from* anywhere."

"I'm Brendan Brackett," he said and held out his palm before she could answer. "I know, I know," he said, "it's a noisy name. Well, I'm a noisy guy."

"You sure are," she said.

"Well, not always," he said.

"I'm Nicky Feldman," she said. "You could get off my desk any time now."

He stayed on the desk and tapped the nameplate that had been made as soon as she'd been hired. Efficiency even in the midst of bureaucracy, Patsy, one of the other secretaries, had said, shaking her head. "I *see* you're Nicky Feldman," Brendan said. "Are you Jewish? I've always felt a great affinity for the Jewish people."

The Living Desert

"No," she said. "Oh, I guess my father was."

"Uh-oh, here comes the boss," he said as Lucille, the main secretary, stepped heavily into the small office. "I'd better not get you into trouble with the boss."

Nicky had lunch at the union with Patsy, whom she'd thought of immediately as Pasty Patsy. Patsy had warned her right away to stay out of the sun. "Arizona has the highest skin cancer rate in the country," she'd said. She applied sun-block lotion and put on a floppy cloth hat before walking Nicky across the quad to the union.

Over their enchilada plates, Patsy told Nicky everybody's history. The college was young, and the buildings seemed to Nicky like prefabricated adobe walls erected for a set. In ten years, though, the faculty had had its carryings-on. One was married to another's ex-wife, who had been his student. The ceramics instructor had lived with the drama professor until he'd had an affair, Patsy said, with the lead in *Streetcar*. Nicky didn't ask, who's he? who's she? what happened? Brendan Brackett had slept with some fifty students, everyone said, and plenty of the faculty too—when the women were younger. But for Nicky, each person stepped into her vision wearing the separate past like a new outfit just picked up at the mall.

Pasty Patsy told her all about her sensitive skin and her boyfriend and her hysterectomy last summer.

The next Monday, Brendan called and asked her to come to his office. She climbed the stairs instead of taking the elevator, and when she reached his office and he said, "Have dinner with me tonight!"—a fifty-year-old boy amazed at the brilliance of his project—Nicky felt winded, unable to ruin his pleasure.

She laughed. "All right," she said. "The noisy man has persuaded me."

"Don't dress up," he said. "This is the desert." He handed her a gracefully sketched map. "Seven okay?"

That evening, he opened the door before she knocked and kissed her on one cheek and then the other. His little house was bright and wild with Indian rugs and painted Mexican carvings and two fervid oils on the wall. He sat her in a Mexican pigskin chair and handed her a glass of wine.

"I *love* all this," Nicky said, waving at the room.

"I've been picking stuff up for years," he said. "One of these days the place is going to O.D. on me."

"It looks spontaneous," she said, "as if you got drunk last night and went crazy with paints."

"Those two oils? They're mine. I've always been into pyrotechnics."

He led her past the futon in his bedroom—"Not to worry," he said—outside to a little courtyard with an empty hot tub and a terra cotta fireplace. He lit the split logs.

"These coals are almost ready," he said and pointed to a hibachi. "But tell me about you while we wait."

Nicky shrugged. "Capricorn. California childhood. Nice mother."

Brendan lifted his eyebrows. "Single white female, likes adventure, is crazy about weird academic types, wants—wants what?"

"Not a thing," Nicky said. And perhaps it was the wine, but that felt correct. Newly born to the desert, what did she want? "Oh, I do want to know the name of that funny tree with the green bark," she said.

"Palo verde," Brendan said. "That's it? That's what you want?"

"No," she said. "I want to name things. All those funny cactuses."

He brought out more wine and a salad with feta cheese and piñon nuts. He laid huge shrimp on the grill.

"You want to name things?" he said.

"I mean learn their names," she said tamely.

While they ate, he talked about the college and the other places he'd taught before and his ex-wife, Alicia.

"A lot of things broke us up," he said. "One major item, maybe I'll tell you sometime. But she quit liking my paintings. Lisha had always loved my paintings and then she quit. Though maybe they changed. Weren't so disgustingly lovable." He dropped another shrimp tail on his plate. "I don't even love them any more. But they're a damn sight better."

Nicky ate the shrimp, half-listening, and felt the pliable night shift and settle on her face and her bare arms.

"You look sad," Brendan said.

"Oh, I'm not," she said. "I was only thinking it's too bad there's no water in your hot tub."

"Well, it's as empty as . . . as you were looking. And it's going to stay drained and empty forevermore."

"How come?" she said, not really wanting to hear his sad past. "Empty just means waiting to be filled. Empty isn't an unpleasant state."

Brendan poked the half-burned logs into the fireplace. "What about your father?" he said. "You have a nice mother, but you didn't tell me about your father."

"That's because there's nothing to tell. He died when I was little, that's all." She stretched. "Oh, I don't like talking about the past. Everybody's all stuffed with their past pains and griefs and how their parents screwed them up. See? That's why we need emptiness."

"I lost my son," Brendan said. "My son was killed. Even after ten years, you don't just pull the plug and drain that out."

She put her hand on his arm. "I'm sorry," she said. She wanted to shake him: after ten years, it's time to shed it. She stroked his arm. "Let's be *here* now."

He stood and pulled her up after him. "I'm sure you've already been given the low-down on Brendan Brackett. But the great lecherous old man is going to thank you for your company now and walk you to your car."

Nicky drove slowly to her apartment. She'd had too much wine. But the streets were empty and she felt alert in the dry night. Her skin felt like thin green bark encasing her emptiness.

For the next week, Nicky felt slightly ashamed, of Brendan for telling so readily about his son's death and of herself for her offer, and she spoke to him formally.

On Thursday, he beckoned her into the hallway. "Hey, you're avoiding me," he said. Students passed them, laden with books and notebooks and portfolios and tool kits, all hurrying or calling to each other, and Nicky thought that she and Brendan couldn't have been more private.

"Yeah, well," she said.

"We're going out tomorrow," he said. "We'll go somewhere this time. Tell me where you live."

"Sorry," Nicky said. "I'm already doing something else." It was true—she and Patsy were going to a movie—but she didn't like the coldness of it. "But maybe another time?" she added. He grinned against the lines of his mustache, and the hint of shame fell away from her.

On Sunday he drove her up the highest mountain in the range north of the city. The foothills were thick with huge saguaros.

"They look so human," Nicky said, and Brendan laughed. "Well, they *do*," she said. "You could almost name them. See, there's Fred, poor guy, he thinks his wife's cheating on him but he knows if he says anything she'll leave him." She pointed to a saguaro with its arms down, slump-shouldered.

"And there's his wife," Brendan said. Her three arms were flung up.

As the switchbacking road rose, the saguaros thinned. Brendan pointed out barrel cactus, yucca, and cholla.

"That's calling jumping cholla," he said.

"You're supposed to let me name it," Nicky said in a mock pout.

"Oh, I forgot. Okay, Adam, what will you name that?" He pointed to a green-yellow cholla that nearly glowed.

"It almost looks soft," Nicky said. "Just hatched. I name it New Chick Cholla."

"It's Teddy-bear Cholla," he said.

"New Chick Cholla," she said.

They rose into grasslands, increasingly scattered with juniper and oak, and at last into pine forest. Near the top they parked and walked among the animal-backed boulders and the pines.

"I used to bring my son up here," Brendan said.

Suddenly Nicky pictured a younger Brendan Brackett and a boy among the pines, and then another picture flashed—more a negative than a photograph: a man and a baby and herself on a beach below a jumbled rock cliff. No, not herself; her young mother. She shook her head.

"You always say 'my son,'" she said.

"Josh," Brendan said. "Joshua."

They followed a stream to a little pool, and Nicky sat on a rock at the edge of the water. Above, the sky was bright fall blue, but within the forest the needles and the rocks and the pines were brown and gray.

The Living Desert

Brendan snapped a picture of her on the rock just above the pool.

"It's too dark," Nicky said. "It won't come out."

"We'll see," he said. "I want to remember you while you're my new-chick cholla."

"I never take pictures," she said. "Besides, I've heard about you and your chicks." She laughed.

It didn't matter, Nicky thought. She was teasing him. She'd never look through his albums and see their photographs. Her mother had black-paged albums with black-and-white photos mounted in white corners, but Nicky hadn't looked at them in years. She didn't know the baby, the toddler, or the child in the pictures, or the man, or even the woman really.

They ate the picnic Brendan had packed and in the late afternoon, with the bright blue sky gone shiny gray, they drove down through the zones.

"Look at that ocotillo," Brendan said. "A poet friend of mine called them 'flagellants of the desert.'"

"What, do they stink?" Nicky said.

"Stink?"

"Well, you said they were the flatulence of the desert," she said.

Brendan laughed and gasped until he had to pull over and wipe his eyes. "Oh God," he said. "Flatulence of the desert. The poet won't think it's so funny, I'll bet."

So it began.

Her mother called two weeks later. "We're still here," she said. "The cat and me. We haven't heard from you for a while."

Nicky could not picture her mother back in California. She could barely recall that the phone was on the kitchen counter.

"Mom," she said, "what are you wearing?"

"Just those old white pants. My blue sweatshirt. What does it matter?"

Then Nicky saw her mother on the barstool, leaning against the wall. She saw the old blue sweatshirt with the cracked baby harp seal on it.

"Mom, there's this man here," Nicky said.

"Oh, I knew it, I knew it," her mother said. "I told Cora my Nicky must have some fellow."

As she described Brendan Brackett for her mother, he took shape—a witty man, an artist, older, sensitive, brilliant, still handsome. She wondered if she loved him.

"Older is all right," her mother said. "Your father was older. But an artist? Well, that's all right. But don't you pose for him."

"Oh Mom," Nicky said. "He's not that sort of artist anyway. If I posed for him, you'd never recognize me."

"Because if you pose for him he'll never marry you. I've read about that too many times."

"We've only gone out a few times. Nobody's talking about getting married," Nicky said. ("I've really fallen for you. I think this is it," Brendan had said last Saturday night from the floor beside his futon. "You didn't have far to fall," she'd said.)

"You know, you could wear my dress," her mother said. "If it comes to it. It'd fit you."

"If it comes to it? Is that hope or desperation?"

"I remember that dress," her mother said sadly. "Cream lace, the whole works. Smash the wine glass. Dance half the night. That band Grandma and Grandpa Feldman hired. The whole works."

"Mom, Mom, don't do that," Nicky said. She couldn't stand to hear—tried not to hear—all the years of her parents' lives.

Brendan gave her an enlargement of the picture he'd taken of her in the pine forest. She was sitting on a brown boulder just above the pool, and all around her the trees and the rocks and the sky were muted brown and gray. Her brown hair and her tan jacket matched the background so that she was almost camouflaged. But the pool was bright blue, fringed with bright green leaves, and in the reflection Nicky's jacket was golden and her hair and face looked brightly out of the blue.

"This is weird," Nicky said. "This is a very strange photo."

"Like the water is a doorway to another world," Brendan said. "That's what I thought right away."

"And this drab world is nothing," she said. "Maybe you ought to paint it."

"I don't do representational," Brendan said stiffly. "I couldn't do anything with that." He tossed the photo to her.

At school they talked politely. Nicky had not told Patsy or any of the others about her and Brendan, and she didn't know if he'd told the other teachers. She framed the photo of her two selves on the rock and in the water and hung it on the wall beside her desk, but she didn't tell anyone that Brendan had taken it. She kept looking at the picture until she felt queasy, and after a week she took it down. It was the present and the past, the bright Nicky and the camouflaged Nicky staring at each other.

At Christmastime, the houses on Brendan's street were strung with thousands of lights, lights climbing the antennas, lights circling the bushes, and in the yards Santas overlooked mangers. The saguaros wore red hats. Brendan had not decorated his house.

"I'm an atheist," he said.

"But I brought you a Christmas present," she said. "I mean, I knew you weren't exactly, uh, pious, but everybody gives Christmas presents." She'd already set her red-ribboned box plainly on his table. "Open it later," she said.

Inside were three pairs of bikini underwear—one tiger striped, one purple with gold trim, one with red hearts. She wished she could take back the intimate, stupid gift.

But he opened the box and laughed. Later he modeled the underwear, posing in the purple pair, with the tiger stripes and the hearts dangling from his ears.

"Gaze upon the royal loins," he said.

She bowed before him. "Hail to the noble purple loins," she said.

"I've really fallen for you," he said. "Do you think you could live forever with these loins?"

Suddenly she remembered the photo of her mother in the wedding dress. She was alone in the picture. Nicky shook her head.

"Why not?" Brendan said. "I've been thinking this was mutual."

"I meant no to something else," she said. "I'm sorry. I know that sounds phony."

"No to what then?"

"Nothing to do with you. Nothing to do with anybody."

He held her, and for an instant she wanted to cry against him for the woman alone in the wedding dress, but then the absurdity of the underwear hanging from his ears made her laugh. Besides, her mother hadn't really been alone at her own wedding.

"I think this might be a proposal," Brendan said. "Think about it. But not right now. Right now you should make obeisance to the royal scepter."

The week before the spring semester began, the secretaries were at work in the underheated offices, but the campus was empty. They all complained about having to work while the professors were still in Puerto Peñasco or somewhere, but they loved their martyrdom and the freedom. Pasty Patsy brought a crockpot of chili one day, and they all took a two-hour lunch at the Pizza Hut another.

"God, this job'd be so great if we didn't have the students or the teachers," Patsy said, and they all laughed.

Nicky thought about telling Patsy that Brendan Brackett had asked her to marry him, and that she just might do it, but she merely listened to the stories of Patsy's inadequate boyfriend and kept Brendan to herself.

When she'd told her mother, she'd said worriedly, "Do you think you know him well enough?"

"Probably not," Nicky had said. And what did it matter? Brendan began on the day he'd taken her up the mountain and they'd named the cacti and he'd taken her picture.

On Thursday night, she drove to his house. *All right*, she would say, *get out the purple shorts and let's celebrate. I say yes.*

She pressed the snout on his brass pig doorbell, and Brendan called, "Oh, you're early, Lisha, but you can come on in." His voice was smugly casual and Nicky knew that even if Alicia was early, he was ready for her.

She turned away. She didn't want to see whatever he had prepared for his ex-wife. She pulled her coat closed. The air was still and cold and thick. She could not marry a man who sucked at his past.

"Alicia?" he called out the door.

"No," she said. No, not Alicia. No, not yours.

"Oh, Nicky," he said. "Well, it's all right. I've just been working. Lisha was just supposed to pick up her old camera. *Now* she decides she wants it back."

"She's here a lot, isn't she?"

"Don't grill me, Nicky," he said.

"You're high, aren't you?"

He pulled her inside.

A naked girl with black hair sat Indian fashion on the couch. The other, a blonde, sat on the floor with her knees up.

"You must be the ex-wife," the girl on the couch said. She leaned her elbows on her spread knees.

Brendan choked, and the choking turned into laughing, and for seconds Nicky watched him spasm as if Alicia and the naked girls inhabited him, all the past and the nubile present writhing inside him. Nicky headed for the door to keep from throwing up in his living room.

"Working—" Brendan choked. "Told you I was working." He picked up the sketchbook and flipped through pages of crayon scribbles. "Girls!" he said. "Assume the position."

The black-haired girl on the couch peered down and stretched her arms out toward the girl on the floor. The blonde turned her face up and stretched her arms out—not to the other girl but toward the ceiling.

Then a woman in torn jeans and a sweatshirt stepped in the front door. "I see you've arranged an audience," she said. "Good old Brenny."

"Oh God," Brendan choked. "Oh God. Why me?"

Abruptly Nicky was furious. "Because you *make* it happen. Because you *need* all this." *Sometimes I think I do things,* Brendan had told her, *so I'll be able to remember them. So I'll have them.* "So let's not whine to God," she said.

The naked girls had dropped their arms, and Alicia was laughing. "Good old Brenny," she said. "Our good old Brenny."

Nicky drove to her apartment. She put on her Garfield nightshirt. She couldn't believe she'd let Brendan entangle her. She lay curled and shaking under the blanket. She thought about calling her mother. Everything was always so nice, she'd say. She thought of her own body floating face up in the green water. She saw her mother running down a gray beach into black water. She saw a huge gray wall of tumbled rocks behind them. She saw the light-gray breakers. The pillowcase under her cheek was wet and cold. Everything was always so nice, she'd say.

She woke to his pounding on her door. She knew in the dark it was Brendan. Then he was hollering her name, and she opened the door lest her neighbors call the police.

"You look so cute. Nightshirt, all tousled," he said. "I'm so sorry. Will you just listen to me? I want to tell you why I'm sorry. And lookie what I brought to help." He pulled a bottle of wine from beneath his sweater. It was the same black sweater he'd been wearing hours ago.

"Just what you need," she said. "More wine."

"It's only wine," he said. "You get glasses."

He was trying to dig out the cork with his pocket knife when she returned with glasses. She took the bottle to the kitchen and used the corkscrew. Her wild reflection looked out of the window like her bright reflection in the water of Brendan's photograph. Which was which, the bright Nicky, the camouflaged Nicky, on which side of the black window?

She sat beside Brendan on the blue plush couch. She knew her hair was wild, her nightshirt childish, her breath bad from sleep. She did not excuse herself to brush her teeth, comb her hair, change her clothes. She and Brendan would stay on one side of the water.

"The reason my hot tub is empty," he said, "is because of my son. My Joshua." His loose hands were on his thighs, and she noticed his dirty nails, crusted with orange and green paint.

"I thought he was in a plane wreck," she said. She looked at the black window behind the slats of the blinds. Who had drowned?

"He was just a kid," he said. "He was fifteen. Fifteen. His friend had just gotten his pilot's license. They went down in the Pinal Mountains. July sixth."

"You told me," she said.

"I know, but. . . . A year afterwards, I decide to have this memorial deal. Alicia's left by then, but I get her back for this, and my father and her sister and some of Josh's friends."

He stopped and drank and sobbed.

"You don't have to tell it," Nicky said.

"Yes, I do. Nobody knows this one. They all think they know what I am, but they don't know this one. Josh had a little girlfriend, Sabrina, just a sweet blonde kid, and she's at this memorial deal. We all tell our favorite Joshua stories and cry, and Lisha and I do a couple lines. And everybody but the little girl leaves. The next thing we're in the hot tub crying for Josh, except I've got my hands on her, those little breasts, her soft stomach, between her legs, and she jumps out and runs inside."

Nicky took a drink. She thought of Brendan's dry hot tub, a pit in his back yard, dead leaves at the bottom.

"I was going to go after her. Get her home at least. Or apologize. Or force her. But I just sat there watching my own gray wormy dick under the water. The next day, I drained the tub."

Nicky eased him down on the couch. She tried to push the cork back in the wine bottle, but it was swollen. She put the extra pillow under Brendan's head and covered him with her blanket.

In the morning, she heard him flush the toilet, but she stayed in bed. When she heard him unchain the lock and then close the door, she got up and made coffee. She called California.

"Good morning, Mama," she said.

Her mother said "Mama?" and right away Nicky saw her at the bedroom phone extension, sitting in her yellow terry bathrobe. Her mother was her mother, and she was a pretty gray-blonde woman in a bright robe, and she was a young woman in a blue and yellow flowered bathing suit on a beach.

"What happened to Daddy?" Nicky said.

"I wondered why you never wanted to know," her mother said.

"I think I remember," Nicky said.

Her mother was silent. Then she said, "I didn't think you did. You were only three."

"You always made everything so nice," Nicky said.

"I thought it would be too traumatic. You were only three. You shouldn't remember."

"I remember the beach," Nicky said. "There was a big rock cliff and the road way above. We had a picnic with Grandma and Grandpa Feldman. Daddy went into the water. You ran back and forth. You had on a flowered suit. Daddy didn't like it. Too much elastic."

"Nicky, he drowned. You always knew that. You've always known he drowned. I couldn't get him. Grandpa couldn't even swim. He got caught in a current, and I couldn't get him."

Her mother was crying, and Nicky saw faces looking into water, and faces looking out of water.

"Come visit me," she said. "Please come. I'll show you this strange desert."

Nicky took her mother to Brendan's show over the lunch hour, when she knew he wouldn't be there. They had barely spoken at school, and Nicky supposed they'd always politely avoid each other's eyes.

At the gallery, past the other artists' Southwest pastels and pseudo-Indian turquoises and tans, they found Brendan's large canvas.

"Well," said her mother, "I don't suppose I should ask what it is."

The colors swirled and splintered.

"I think it's the sky and a reflection of the sky," Nicky said. In the splintered circle of gray sky and brown branches above, and of bright blue water and green leaves below, Nicky believed she saw a shadow woman with her arms held out to a yellow shape in the water.

"I guess I don't get it," her mother said.

"Maybe because you always did know where you're from," Nicky said.

"What does that mean?" her mother said. "We're from California."

"I'm from you and Daddy," Nicky said.

"Well, of course you are."

"It's weird," Nicky said. "Somehow I always felt like everything's an exhibit in some museum that closes as soon as I leave it."

"We should have talked about your father all along. I should have told you what it was like in that cold water, how he looked when they finally brought him back to the beach and laid him on the sand. It was windy and the sand stuck to his wet skin." Her mother was crying. "I'll never forget how he looked, all bluish-gray and shiny."

There was no emptiness, Nicky thought. Everything was invisibly present.

She didn't know if Brendan had painted himself and his son and

Alicia and little blonde Sabrina in the canvas, if he had let the guilts brim over and now might be replenished.

"It must have been awful to keep it to yourself," Nicky said.

"I always thought it'd be better," her mother said. "And you never asked."

"I want to know about it all now," Nicky said. "Everything before, too."

In the painting, she saw the bright shape beneath the surface holding its arms straight up, knowing that the past sat there on the gray rock, and knowing now how to live in the blue water.

The Night of the Child

SOMETHING is wrong with me. I am drinking rosé, terrible sweet wine, as I do on Friday night, abstaining on weeknights, and the headache is here. I am taking Tylenol Extra-Strength capsules in the full knowledge that this past week a woman in New York died from cyanide-laced Tylenol Extra-Strength capsules. In the probable knowledge that rosé and Tylenol do not mix anyway.

In the full knowledge.

Of Christmas.

He is in the bedroom with *his* drink which is Jim Beam, and he does not suggest I come lean against the pillows beside him. He has cleaned his cat's infected ears—alone, which isn't easy, given the cat's furiously uncontrollable back legs when the ear is stimulated—and he did not say please hold these goddamn legs and stay out of my light while you do it. He does not say where's the clean sheets didn't you do the laundry today why are there dog prints all over these sheets? He does not say here I am in my happi coat come take it off me.

It is Christmas but we have to keep telling ourselves here in the tropics.

Once I was a child in Michigan. My sisters and I loved babies. As soon as we each turned thirteen, we were allowed to baby-sit, though I know I wouldn't now allow any thirteen-year-old child to tend a baby of mine. If I had a baby. But even then we loved the soft spot on the scalp, the bloated face of a baby. I loved diapers even. We were just girls in Michigan and a year, Christmas to Christmas, could no more be measured than snowflakes. That thirteenth Christmas I was invited—invited!—to play my French horn with the cornets in the Congregational Church's Christmas Eve service. We rehearsed in the young people's meeting room in the church basement every day after school, and I was replete with our great noise and everybody's babies and the Christ Child.

What we should do, I told my sisters, is adopt a baby. They were only eleven and twelve. I was nearly fourteen. There are babies who don't have parents and homes and Christmases, I said. And we ought to adopt one of them.

Our town wasn't really large, but it had its orphanage, and we called it up. I said I was Mrs. Gerald Warner, who was our mother, and I wanted to see if there was a baby who wasn't going anywhere for Christmas.

"Well, Mrs. Warner," someone with an official voice said, "we don't have babies here. What did you say your name was?"

"Gerald Warner," I said. "I mean, Mrs. Gerald Warner."

"Well, but what's *your* name?"

"Annie. Anna, I mean." I had to think. It was only my father who called her Annie.

"Listen, Miss Annie Warner, we don't have babies per se. But, you know, there are some children who won't be going anywhere for Christmas. Why don't you talk this over with your mother?"

"How little?"

"Some as young as six."

It wasn't diapers and bibs and baby bottles. But I supposed it was little enough.

Mrs. Gerald Warner was amused, probably even touched. She drove us to the orphanage and we picked ourselves out a little girl, the littlest girl. Her name was Elaine and she would be ours for Christmas.

I didn't know what our father thought about it. I don't know now. Perhaps he took to the bedroom alone and didn't say Annie come lean against the pillows with me.

We were each given five dollars to spend on Elaine. The relatives were informed, and boxes from Texas and Massachusetts each included a little package for Elaine. I bought her a book, *Hurry Home, Candy*, which had made me cry when I was young. I did not think who would read it to her. I thought *I* would pull her to my side of the couch and read her the story of the puppy hit with the broom and lost in the swollen creek and tempted, scared and starving, to a kind man's food, and we would weep together, the orphan and I. I do not remember what my sisters bought her. On Christmas my sisters and I had more boxes, I remember, and Santa Claus left a higher stack beneath our chairs and plaid coats. But Elaine had her stack, too, and her boxes. And, after all, she was only six.

Jeff and I have no babies. It has been oh years of Friday-night rosé, years of Jim Beam, years of adequate marriage. We have no babies. It is Christmas and we hang our stockings from the tails of plastic cat and dog models. It is Christmas and we can allow corny plastic cat and dog models into our tasteful living room. On Christmas morning the stockings will be full of sample after-shave and perfume, of typewriter correction tape, of little airline bottles, of see-through panties and paperback books and Mr. Boston's Bar Guide. There will be boxes and boxes under the tree, for we love Christmas, boxes from Texas and Massachusetts and Michigan and each other. We tape the Christmas cards to the door frames. We burn bayberry candles. The mistletoe tacked to the ceiling is plastic, for the real thing is poisonous to cats.

All of us, all but Dad anyway, went to the orphanage to get Elaine two days before Christmas. In our car coats and snow boots, we waited in the hot hallway while Elaine was brought to us out of the old house. The floors were varnished and there was a long striped runner down the hallway. There was a table with a homemade mailbox with slots for all the girls. Elaine had a slot, but we did not know who sent her mail. Now we would send her cards and letters. There was no one in the hot old house.
"I didn't think they'd have a Christmas tree," I said. But in the high-ceilinged room off the hallway where we waited stood a huge tree with bubble lights that were bubbling even though there was no one left in the orphanage two days before Christmas.
"I don't think they're all really orphans," I said. "Or why'd they all be gone?"
"Maybe," Mother said, "there are others like my girls who are thinking about them."
My favorite Christmas show had always been *The Little Match*

Girl. If I couldn't *be* that mistreated child lighting her last matches to warm her own fingers, rubbing a peephole on the frosted glass and watching the party within—the candles, the fireplace, the presents, the family—then I'd be the one to open the door and take her into the warmth.

Elaine began crying before we were halfway to the shopping center. We'd been going to give her money to buy presents, thinking she'd be ashamed to receive and not give. But we couldn't take her crying into Woolworth's. I'd been planning to ask for Dilly Bars at the ice-cream booth, knowing my mother was a Christmas pushover and imagining the new thrill of the Dilly Bar to Elaine.

We didn't know what to do.

Mother pulled over to the curb and leaned over the seat as she did when my sisters were squabbling in the back seat, and for an instant I was afraid she'd slap at Elaine.

"What is it, dear?"

Elaine was a pudgy little girl with hair too short for us to put in curlers. She wore red pants that still had the firm fuzzy nap of new corduroy. She didn't say anything, just sobbed quietly beside me. When I baby-sat, I'd always distract the criers with games or a story or a bedtime snack, authorized or not.

"Maybe she'd like a Dilly Bar," I suggested. "We could all get Dilly Bars at the shopping center."

"Why don't you ask *her*?" Mom said.

"Would you?" I said, looking down at the orphan beside me. I didn't want to embarrass her by looking right into her red face. Maybe she didn't even know what a Dilly Bar was. "It's ice cream," I told her. "Wouldn't you like a nice ice cream bar?"

Finally we just went home. "Maybe it's better to settle in anyway," Mom said. "Too many new people, the crowds, all that excitement—it might be too much anyway."

"Now she won't get to sit on Santa's lap," one of my sisters said.

At last Elaine stopped crying and talked a little. We played Chinese checkers with her. The day before Christmas we went sledding at the golf course, and I got her to sit in front of me on the toboggan so I could put my arms around her and tell her not to be scared, and she even laughed on the second run. At night she got to share my double bed, since my sisters already shared a room and anyway she'd been my idea. We sat up in bed and I read her Christmas stories until she fell asleep, and when she wet the bed Christmas Eve I didn't care. I didn't even wake Mom, just put a towel on her side of the bed and got a clean sheet from the hall closet.

Jeff and I live in the tropics. On an island. Expensive brown Christmas trees are sold in parking lots. The downtown streets are hung with sun-faded red bunting and tongueless bells. In the day, the sky's lucid blue seems to await Easter more than Christmas.

Now at night I carry my glass of rosé outside and wade through the grass that eternally needs cutting, stamping to shake the mosquitoes from my bare legs. The headache is wadded inside my skull like supersaturated snow clouds above the midwest. The surf does not sound like the rush of snow. I cannot locate the Southern Cross in the shiny black sky.

The dog howls politely inside the house. I let her out and she squats beside the banana tree. "Bedtime, pups," I tell her. "Let's go to bed." Already there will be two cats on the bed, I know.

Jeff is holding a paperback but his eyes are closed. "She's done her duty," I say. "May we come to bed with you?"

"Mother may I," he says.

I lean against him. "I think we need children," I say.

"Yeah? Tell the tadpole factory to start putting out live bait."

"We could adopt," I say. I look down, not wanting to embarrass him by peering into his Jim Beam eyes, or not wanting to see the here-we-go-again eyes rolled up.

"Children do not save you," he says.

On Christmas Eve, we drove to the First Congregational Church. My French horn was in its black case in the trunk. As we waited at the light on Lovell Street, a station wagon going the other way hit a dog. I saw the dog tumble beneath the car, tumbling under the car for half a block before the station wagon shook it free.

At the church, I sat with the cornets across from the choir. *We three kings of Orient are*, we played, and the three robed kings filed down the center aisle with the measured steps of bridesmaids.

The Night of the Child

Those paces, the muted then open brass, the dog tumbled beneath the station wagon, the orphan sitting with my parents and watching me play—all quickened my heart, and I was swollen with unshed tears and full knowledge of the night of the child.

On Christmas morning, my sisters and I woke up before Elaine did. We got her up and showed her what to do: we all crawled into our parents' bedroom to the foot of their bed, worked our hands under the covers, and pulled their big toes.

Downstairs we weren't allowed to touch the stockings or the boxes that Santa had left beneath our coats, not until the Christmas records were stacked on the turntable and the coffee was perking.

"Youngest first," Dad proclaimed. "That's the little girl in the pink nightgown, I believe."

Elaine turned her stocking upside down to dump everything out. I showed her how to pull things out one at a time. You had to examine each toy. You had to exclaim. Elaine was a quiet little girl, but we all exclaimed some for her.

After we'd all done the stockings, we did the Santa stacks beneath our coats. While we sorted and examined the books and games and clothes, Mom made waffles.

Elaine had her little stack of presents from Santa: a nurse kit, a Betsy Wetsy with two outfits, a Chutes and Ladders, and a red sweater. "How come it ain't wrapped?" she asked.

We exchanged looks at the *ain't*. "Because it's from Santa Claus," I said.

"At home he wraps them," she said. She meant *at the home*.

We ate the Christmas waffles with powdered sugar.

"I think someone's too excited to be very hungry," Dad said.

But Elaine was crying again.

"What? What is it?" we asked.

"The excitement," Mom said.

I thought it was Christmas, family, waffles with powdered sugar, stockings and presents: her awareness of her orphanhood.

"It tastes funny," she said, holding a piece of waffle up on her fork. "We never eat it like this."

So Mom brought out the syrup and got Elaine a new plate and a clean waffle.

Dad turned over the records and we began then on the wrapped presents beneath the tree. We handed them out one at a time, unwrapping and ritually exclaiming, until at last there was nothing under the tree but the felt skirt hiding the stand and we were glutted.

Mom went to tent the turkey with foil, Dad to burn the wrappings outside, my sisters to begin trying on their new clothes for the modeling show. I sat with Elaine on the floor, replete with wealth and ritual.

"What do you like best?" I asked her. She'd probably say the Betsy Wetsy, I thought, but I was almost fourteen and I knew that someday she'd look back at all the warmth and remember *Hurry Home, Candy* and me who read it to her, and think of herself as the little dog timidly creeping toward the human's outstretched hand.

"You all got more," Elaine said.

"Why," I said, "how ungrateful can you get? Here we take you in and give you all this stuff and you can't even say thank you. All you can say is 'you got more,'" I mimicked. I scooped up my pile of new clothes and stalked away from her, upstairs to join my real sisters and the fashion show.

She sat alone in the living room beside her presents, crying for a while before anyone found her. She didn't tell on my meanness. Eventually she opened the nurse's kit and used the stethoscope on the doll. My sisters dressed her up in her new clothes and put her through the paces. At bedtime she began crying again because we had toothpaste, not tooth powder. The day after Christmas she said she wanted to go home, even though she was supposed to stay three more days, and Mom and Dad drove her back to the orphanage and carried in her new clothes and her toys in shopping bags. I never did read her the book I'd bought for her. I don't know if anybody ever did or if she finally read it to herself. I don't know if she even kept it.

Months later, she called our house and asked Mom for twenty-five dollars. Mom said there was giggling in the background and she figured some of the other kids put her up to it. "We really ought to have her over again," Mom said. But we never did.

The following Christmas, I was nearly fifteen, and though I still loved babies, I had my secret shame of renouncing Elaine and my adolescent certainty that nothing ever lived up to itself.

The Night of the Child

★

"Sweetheart," Jeff says, "you always get maudlin at Christmas. Especially when you're drinking wine."

"You love Christmas, too," I accuse him. "Who always wants to open everything Christmas Eve? Who always buys champagne for when we decorate the tree? And that's not it, anyway." I am crying, and I defiantly turn to him so he'll know it.

"Jesus," he says. "I can't talk to you when you're drinking."

On Christmas Eve we carefully fill each other's stocking. We stand outside together while the dog does her duty. I point to the three stars of Orion's Belt, the only constellation I recognize. I have not put my lips to the mouthpiece of a French horn in years.

On Christmas morning, I make walnut stuffing and put the turkey in the oven before we begin with our stockings. After we've opened all the presents, one by one, I make French toast and Jeff makes Bloody Marys, and we eat the French toast with powdered sugar instead of syrup and afterwards stir our Bloody Marys with stalks of celery and comment on the presents my sisters and everybody sent us across the sea. We both love Christmas and we love each other. We unwrap the dog's rawhide and the cats' Christmas catnip for them. I model my new pink bathing suit and pose beside the Christmas tree for Jeff to take my picture.

"Knockers up," he says.

I put my hand on my naked hip and grin, satisfied and alone, self-banished in the tropical winter.

Safeway

"Hey, Tina," Marie said at the next register, "get a load." I like Marie. She doesn't call me Teeny like most everyone else does, including my own father. All right, so I'm short. So I'm scrawny. "Just a little bit of nothing," my dad says. And it isn't a compliment.

Marie jerked her head to the row of carts. A woman was trying to pull the first cart loose. It must have been jammed. She had a flock of pale kids around her. It was hard to see how many. But I could see the mother, all right.

"A load is right," I said.

The woman was fat. I don't just mean plump or overweight, like most middle-aged women. I should know. I'm here beeping through those twin-packs of chips and the white wax bags from the bakery counter every Saturday, eight hours every blessed Saturday. Don't tell me they don't nosh down half those maple frosted longjohns before they're out of the parking lot. I should know: my own mother's an overweight middle-aged woman.

But this woman fighting with the carts was about ten pounds shy of the circus. She was wearing red polyester Bermudas with the elastic waist and a green stretch sleeveless top—tucked in, yet. Her huge bosom—which was the only word for it, there couldn't have been actual breasts—and her huge belly were separated by the red elastic waistband of the shorts, and her rear stuck out practically to the day-old bread rack. She looked like a giant Christmas ornament.

"Some eyeful," the old guy at my register said.

I ran his cat food over the scanner, can by can. Bleep. *Thirty-four,* the computer said. *Thirty-four. Thirty-three.* I always wonder why the voice is a woman's. They could have made it a nice male

Safeway

voice. Instead it's a thin-lipped female. I've decided that the company's psychology team has figured that all those middle-aged women in their Bermudas wouldn't respond as well. You might think they'd rather hear some nice man's voice. But maybe they'd rather not think of men and food at the same time. There isn't any judgment in that female machine's voice.

The old guy had three bags of egg noodles after the cat food, then a pound block of margarine and a half-gallon of milk. I hoped he didn't have any flour at home. I hoped he wasn't going to cook up a white sauce, stir in that Savory-Supper Tuna, and serve it over the noodles.

"You must have a lot of cats," I said, hoping it was so.

Suddenly from the direction of the carts a kid screamed. Everyone stopped moving. The circus lady was still yanking on a stuck cart, and one of her kids had a finger caught. She let go and yanked the kid's hand out. He kept on screaming, holding up his hand. Nobody moved. The woman slapped the kid's mouth. "Shut up, Rodney," she said. "Don't be a goddamn crybaby."

The silence into which she'd spoken eased up then. Scanners started bleeping, computer women began enunciating, and Rodney wound down.

The old guy's frozen cheesecake came up after the milk.

"That sure looks good," I said. Usually, I don't comment on people's food. I think they were embarrassed, really, at the things winging around the conveyor—little tins of anchovies, economy size boxes of Tampax, a single carrot in one of the free plastic bags. And they hardly ever watch their stuff moving along, as if it has nothing to do with them. *They* certainly aren't going to drink that beer or whonk down that bag of home-style soft chocolate chip cookies or wipe with that pink-flowered toilet paper. But I was glad the old guy could afford a Sara Lee. The evening's entree probably wasn't noodles à la kitty tuna. Still, I'd have felt better if he'd had a bag of litter in his cart.

"That isn't nothing," Charlie said, poking his nose in the direction of the fat woman. Then he said, "Plastic or paper?" to the old guy and started bagging. I wonder why carry-outs always have to be named Charlie. I wonder what their parents thought with the newborn son: Hmm, yes dear, you're right, this one's destined to be a carry-out, we'd better name him Charlie.

"So you should have seen Fatty in the parking lot," Charlie whispered to me and the old guy. "I'm out there rounding up carts, right? 'Git along, little dogies,' I'm singing, and one of the brats laughs a little bit. Like none of them had cracked a grin in six months. All of a sudden she's slapping the kid to Sunday and back, I mean hard and not just on his spank cushion, either, and the kid's just hollering."

"Somebody ought to report a mother like that," my old guy said.

The red and green monster and her brood rounded the corner and headed up aisle 2, housewares and pet food. The four kids, three boys and a girl, were pale—sallow was more like it—in limp, wan shorts and shirts. They were barefoot.

I looked over at Marie, and she just shook her head.

My next one was a young mother, practically my age, I guessed, with her baby in an infant seat propped on the front of the cart. She was chewing gum, like a cow pulling its foot in and out of the mud, as my mother would say. She had a box of that you're-worth-it hair coloring, a case of Similac, two frozen pizzas, and a huge box of disposable diapers. I've always wondered if my parents had to get married. I know they were too young, especially my mother, and my father had quit college after the first year. But of course there's no asking. What makes you ask that? my mother would say. What would make you think such a thing? And what would there be for me to say about the way the coldness of their house makes me want to shiver.

"You little pea-brain, what in the hell do you think you're doing?" The monster was all the way at the end of the store, by the dairy case, it sounded like. The whole store could hear her. Strangers were exchanging glances and shaking their heads. "You goddamn little son of a bitch," we heard, and then the kid's wail.

Charlie said, "Well, if he's a little son of a bitch, we know what that makes her."

"I really can't believe I'll ever do that way to my Scottie," the young mother said.

All the way through the store, up and down the aisles, soups and vegetables, coffee and flour, picnic supplies and facial tissue, she yelled at her children and hit them. At the end of the snacks aisle,

Safeway

the oldest boy tried to put a bag of caramel corn in the cart, and I saw her pound on his head. That boy would never be able to eat caramel corn if somebody gave it to him even two years from now, I thought, never get that gummy stuff stuck on his teeth and suck it off like kids do. Well, let's not get mushy, I told myself. The worst thing that's going to happen to this kid is *not* that he'll forever hate caramel corn. It was like the time my mother made a tuna casserole for supper, and my father took a look at the casserole and said, "I think I'll just make me a ham sandwich." My mother didn't even cry, and I sat and ate and ate that meal, but I'd probably barf if you put a tuna casserole before me now.

The monster wheeled her cart up to my line. She was a half-dozen people back. "Rodney, I swear to God you're even dumber than your brother." I heard the slap and then the kid's crying. I wondered why they hadn't learned to keep their distance. I supposed they would, given time. All four kids had runny noses and snail trails down their cheeks from crying. Kids have no choice but to home in on whatever parents they're given.

My next lady was middle-aged, which I knew my mother wasn't really, not yet. I breezed her week's worth of Weight-Watchers' frozen dinners across the scanner, and it gave polite bleeps. *Two fifty-seven,* the computer woman said. *Three twenty-nine.*

"If she writes a check," I said to the lady, "I'm going to copy down her name and address. I'm going to report her to the police for child abuse."

I wanted to see what this lady in her navy pants and plaid blouse would say, this lady who was at least trying.

"Henrietta, you don't quit that I'm going to smack you," the red and green monster said. I never could see what the kids were doing, except when the one picked up the caramel corn. Then she smacked Henrietta, who turned toward the candy and gum rack to cry.

The plump lady nodded at me. "I would," she said. "Some people shouldn't be allowed to have children."

I wondered what my own mother would say. You can't always know how it will turn out, she might say. When you're a kid, you can't know you'll end up living in a refrigerator, middle-aged before you're forty, cold and curdled as cottage cheese. She'd probably say to mind my own beeswax, hadn't I enough to worry about without borrowing other folks' trouble?

When the monster mother got to me, I bleeped through her bread and her soda, her bologna and her cans of gravy.

"Don't never have no kids," she told me. She laughed. The smallest boy was still twitching with the after-effects of crying. Henrietta looked at me blankly. I couldn't know what her home was like.

The mother handed over bills, not a check. Before I gave her the change, I turned to Marie. "Hey, ring me up four Hersheys," I said, and handed her the quarters I'd had in my pocket. I was supposed to take home a carton of sour cream for whatever casserole my mother was making for supper. I didn't care. I didn't care about eating.

Let them call me Teeny. Teensy-tinesy Tina. I wondered if I'd been as caved-in, as dead pale as Henrietta when I'd been little. I did not know if we three had ever flopped on the ground together on a blanket and eaten a fat picnic, in love with fried chicken and deviled eggs together. I only remembered bodies in stiff dining room chairs, canned green beans passed along, my father's insurance papers spread at the left of his plate. "Here you are, Teeny," he'd say. "A little bit of nothing like you better down some of these green beans."

I reached over the check-out counter and handed each kid a Hershey's bar. They took them stupidly.

"All right, shit-for-brains, what do you say?" the mother said. Her right hand was ready.

"Thank you, lady," Henrietta whispered.

"You're a sweetheart," I told her. "You remember that."

The automatic doors opened for the monster just the same as for everyone, check-out girls and carry-out boys, teenaged mothers, old men, and all the middle-aged women with their families' groceries. I was no lady, and Henrietta was probably nobody's little sweetheart. And it probably mattered that the coldness which she would wear next to her skin was not the same as mine.

I thought of her eating the chocolate I'd given her, and abruptly I was hungry. There was nothing for us to do but make our own heat from the inside out. There is nothing for us but to grow up, clothed in coldness, our hearts fired.

The Pressure to Modulate

ALL during the concert she held her secret. The imported violinist did the Barber violin concerto, weaving with passion, and Emily looked through the lights at all the dark heads of the audience. At intermission, all the minks and the false teeth sipped from plastic cups of wine. After each movement of the symphony, at the shotgun applause and the shushing, Rosellen next to her said, "Idiots," and shook the spit out of her horn. None of them, propped in rows in the dark, knew they were dead. "What's with you tonight, Em?" Rosellen said. Emily thought about whispering, None of you—except Mozart and me—know we're all dying. She felt her furious moist secret beating.

At home David had the news on and a whiskey at his side. "How'd it go? Old Clyde get the requisite ovations? Betsy called. Wants you to send her long blue dress. She said you'd know. Wants me to send cash."

Emily turned off the television.

"Hey," David said and picked up the remote.

"I may have cancer," she said.

He held his arm out, the remote control pointed at the television.

"Oh, why do we always have to wear black?" Emily said. "Excuse me while I go slip into something a little more comfortable. A shroud or something."

When she returned to the living room, the weatherperson was predicting more rain and reciting flash flood warnings, and David stood and put his arms stiffly around her. "Tell me how you want me to react," he said. "Tell me what you want me to do."

★

Even in high school, Emily had been second horn. For two years she'd sat beside Dave Ballinger, the first horn, and when far into their senior year he'd said to her, "I think we have a neat platonic relationship," she'd hurried to the library after orchestra to look it up, hopeful but not really believing the great Dave Ballinger was going to ask her out, and then walked to her seat in chemistry, late, a mouthpiece indentation still on her mouth and in her head *Platonic love: an intimate companionship between a man and a woman which is characterized by the apparent absence of sexual desire.*

But then years later, another David had fallen in love with her. In her long black dress she'd walked out into the temperate night with her black horn case hitting her knee with every step. "Please," a man said, "I ain't nothing but a ignorant reporter and I need help." He was black haired, and he wore a white snap-front shirt with red roses embroidered on the yoke. For the first years he kept it as his symphony shirt, and by the time he'd filled out and the shirt stretched too tight across the shoulders, he'd quit going to all the concerts. He wanted nothing from Emily in the first dark but help with the review he had to write for the *Prospector*. She went with him to a campus coffee house and sat outside, and he took notes beneath colored lights that slicked on her black dress.

"What did it mean?" he asked. "The music."

"There wasn't any program," she said.

"Well, I had one." He pulled the folded brochure from his back jeans pocket.

"No," she said, "I mean it wasn't program music. There wasn't any story or particular scenes." It had been Mahler's Fifth, before anybody much except the Philharmonic was doing Mahler, and she didn't think it had been just right. For the first two movements they'd sounded like a high school marching band. But then in the third movement she and the other horns had raised their bells and all the music had swarmed over them like fire.

"It's 'only' music," she said. "Bruno Walter said that, not me. Just pure music."

He'd written his review for the college paper and in another year he'd married his older woman and gone to work for the *Daily Observer*. She'd always thought people must wonder why he'd married her, she was so plain. He was moody and she spent too much time in rehearsal and at the middle school, leading the kids through yet another Elgar or something. Their children had grown up loved and, she thought, somehow a bit neglected. Always she and David had been the center of each other's life. You are the love of my life, he said. They were ordinary. He was a newspaperman—"Don't call me a journalist," he said—and they simply lived their ordinary lives in the desert. She wasn't talented but she worked hard, satisfied to sit in the midst of the fire, and she was the love of David's life. Nobody else, not even their children, knew theirs was the love of the century.

On Friday she tried to cry. Cancer, cancer, she thought, but before she could cry she had to eat breakfast and then go buy a little present to add to the box for her daughter.

"What are you, schizophrenic?" the clerk said when she handed him the two CDs—a Megadeth and a Brahms.

She laughed. "My daughter. I give her what she wants. But I still try to convert her. My son's the same way. Except there's no hope of conversion there."

She'd never really cared. The music, the hair, the friends—David had done battle, but she'd wanted only peace. At rehearsal, her friends ranted about their kids' electric guitars and drums and noise. "They don't know anything," Rosellen had said, years ago. "Jess wouldn't even know how to read music except that I had at him when he was too young to fight it. They don't know anything about counterpoint or tone color or the pressure to modulate, nothing."

"Let it go," Emily'd said. "They'll come to it. Or they won't. In the meanwhile, you've got it."

In the meanwhile, Rosellen became principal horn and her son, Jess, disappeared in Nashville. In the meanwhile, Betsy and Eric squabbled and got into minor trouble and took good degrees, and all the while Emily was the love of David's life.

Before she could cry on Friday, she had to get Betsy's box to the post office, and then she had two private lessons. She had time to cry before David got home, and she put on the Mahler Ninth for priming, but it was no go.

★

After the biopsy on Wednesday morning, she felt fragile, carrying some tentative thing that shouldn't be jarred, yet also vigorous.

On the table, she'd had to keep stopping her fingers from playing at her side. Tap-tap-tap tap-tap on the paper, a little Handel, tap-tap tap-tap-tap, and then some Bach. She'd wiped her sweaty hands and torn the wet paper. She'd pressed her spread hands on her chest—*this is my body*.

But on the way out, she thought the worst was over, it was all a mistake. She stopped and bought a pair of Reeboks, and then put them on in the recital hall's parking lot. Inside, at practice, everybody said, oh you've got new shoes. Emily walked cushioned and springy through the rest of the day.

At night she told David, "I think I overreacted." She was still springy.

"Maybe you did," he said, "and maybe you didn't."

When she woke Sunday morning, David was already up. She put on her robe and blundered through the house for him. He'd left the Sunday paper, still in its plastic bag, by the front door. He'd made coffee.

"David?" she said. "Where's the love of my life?" She never called him that.

On Sundays they always drank coffee and read the paper in bed. Sometimes she brought breakfast in on a big wooden tray. Want to play my horn? he'd say.

She opened the front door. It was raining again, and the desert yard was furred with green. His car was gone.

He'd left the note by the Mr. Coffee. *Forgot to tell you: have to cover some deal downtown. Back by noon. Love, husband.*

She carried the paper and a big mug of sweetened coffee back to bed and sat propped up. The rain let up and the early sky silvered over. Cover some deal on Sunday morning. He'd said love, yes. He was dutiful. She thought of her tissue sample blackening under some microscope. Now she was sick. The cells were wild inside her, mating furiously, metastasizing in her soft organs.

She was still in bed when David unlocked the front door. He came into the bedroom in his jeans and black sweater. He looked like somebody else, dark-haired, a broad-shouldered man who might kiss some woman and lower himself onto her. He held a McDonald's bag.

"I'm not hungry," she said. He was no husband.

"Well, that's good. Because this is just an empty bag."

"Oh," she said. Her cells beat on the inside of her skin. "Oh, well."

"I figured you'd eat. I figured you'd be up."

"I don't want to move. I feel like I'll jar the cancer loose and it'll go spreading all inside me."

"I don't think it works quite like that," he said. "But stay put. Take it easy."

"You don't have to sound so cheerful." She lifted the covers, but he didn't move, and so she leapt out of bed and yanked on her sweats. "What on earth did you have to cover on Sunday morning?"

"Oh. The homeless. That tent city across from St. Anthony's. You think it's easy downing two Egg McMuffins after that?"

"But you do your duty, don't you?"

In the afternoon she walked the house with a notebook, listing paintings' values, noting who'd given what objects, willing things to Betsy and Eric.

"This is melodramatic, I know," she said. "It's not as if I'm going to head for the big orchestra in the sky tomorrow."

He laughed. "No," he said. "But I'll bet they've got one hell of a harp section. They'll be glad of a horn."

In high school she used to carry her lunch instead of eating at the cafeteria. She'd reserve one of the practice rooms behind the stage, do the real practicing first and then eat her sandwich and apple, pretending to study the music propped on the black stand in case anybody looked through the glass. The indentation of the mouthpiece on her lips would be almost faded by fifth period. The few times she tried going to the cafeteria, she'd carried her orange tray with the steaming casserole, little milk carton, and Jell-O around the room, waiting for somebody to call, "Hey Emily! Come sit with us over here." Finally she'd have to ask formally if she could join some group or she'd crouch alone at the end of a table and swallow a few of the slimed noodles. She'd hide in a practice room for weeks of lunches after that.

Her own children had friends, platonic and otherwise. At ten, Eric had said in the middle of Safeway that he wanted a male candy bar. The one with nuts, he said. There'd been sleepovers and curfew battles and basketball. Her children, inside their spangled skin, hadn't needed to hide.

In the tiny closed room that reeked of peanut butter, she might as well have been a stone. Sitting on a metal chair before the heavy black music stand, touching the fading mouthpiece circle, she'd thought of stones turned and turned in flooded washes. She'd thought of her organs smooth and gray inside her plain skin.

She could not then foresee David Westerman, wearing embroidered roses, finding her in the dark. She knew she'd go to the state university and major in music. But she did not see that she would ever connect, ever be fixed in anybody's life, ever sit quickened and pliant as the music flickered around her.

Now if she died, Betsy and Eric would fly back and cry and eat the casseroles some of the brass section would bring to the house. She closed her eyes and her funeral went black. She'd tell David to cremate her. Maybe Rosellen could play something. She thought of tears running straight down Rosellen's face, following the grooves to her mouth and ruining her embouchure. She'd need a spittoon to empty the spit valve. The kids would fly right away. Emily's death would be a flicker in all their lives.

But David would sit in his chair at night and click from channel to channel. He wouldn't eat. He'd be silent, and later he might put his hand into the box of her ashes and finger her bone shards and then wipe his hand across his face. He would think about taking the box down into the dry wash behind the house. He would write dry stories for the *Daily Observer* and go gray and turn to stone without her.

Last year Clyde had decided to do the Mahler Second. "Maybe he has a thing for you," Rosellen had said. "Does he know what a Mahler freak you are? I can hardly believe it, the way he always goes for the blue-hair special."

"It's not the Ninth, with all that death, though," Emily said. "With the Second you've got your nice resurrection."

"Your loud resurrection."

Now she thought of the music's terror, the spurting graves, the streaming dead.

She thought of her own body slid into the fire, incinerated to powder and slag.

The alto in the fourth movement had sung like a child of primal light. But the last movement roared into immortality, no tepid light but the fire itself. Emily had been one of the offstage horns, calling from beyond.

She called the clinic Monday exactly at 10:30 when the report was due back from pathology. "We just got these in," the receptionist said. "They aren't sorted and nobody's looked at them. Your doctor will call you."

She thought she'd have to call from school between lessons. But he called in ten minutes.

"No malignancy," he said.

"Really? I've been getting ready to die all weekend. Really?"

"Straight scoop. Anyway, I doubt very much you'd have died."

First she bent over with her face on her knees and cried, loudly, with no accompaniment. Then she called the school and cancelled. "I'm taking a sick day," she told the secretary. She put on her new Reeboks and ran down the street until it angled near the wash, and then she ran in the sand, taking giant grotesque steps, back toward the house.

"Look out, all you javelinas," she yelled. "Out of my way, you coyotes."

David came in at dusk. "I tried to call you. It's supposed to rain again."

"It's perfectly clear out," Emily said. She dished bean soup from the crock pot. "Come on, sit down."

"The news has rain coming at us from that California storm."

"You'd rather believe the news than the sky," she said. She sat across from him at the little kitchen table. "So you called to tell me it's supposed to rain?" She giggled. She was alive. Later on she might tease him a little more.

He looked up quickly with a spoonful before his mouth, as if she might be hysterical.

"No," he said. "The biopsy. What'd you find out?" He spooned in the beans.

"I'm clean. No malignancy."

His eyes closed for an instant and then he looked at her. He resumed chewing the mouthful of beans.

She heard the long note at the beginning of the Ninth, the long pain held past endurance, the note she'd always thought was the knowledge of oncoming death and all the world that would go out, with nothing, blank nothing beyond its sand and its cactus flowers and its mountains and its floods and its lovers. This is ridiculous, she thought, their eyes caught as he chewed. Modulate already. They held and held. Then she watched his hand put down his spoon. She heard the pain of the bow torn across the strings.

"Well, that's great," David said. "That's a big relief."

In their knowledge, they sat together for the evening, watching television, reading. "Oh, here's a letter from your son," she said at some point. "They're sending him to Germany for some conference."

"You could go along. The land of your beloved Gustav."

"He was Austrian."

"Close enough."

"Do you want to read the letter?" she said.

She thought of telling him the next day that there'd been a mistake in the pathology report. When old Richard Norton in the trombones had finally decided to leave his wife, she'd come down with cancer and he'd had to stay and see her through it to her death. That was one way to hold your man, she thought. Their friends the Klampers were about to split after Bert told Sandra he was in love with someone else when she came down with pregnancy. Bert stayed until the baby grew all the way up but then he did it anyway.

The ten o'clock news warned of increased rain in the early hours and possible flash floods. "Increased rain?" she said. "It isn't raining at all." She stepped outside in her stocking feet and shut the door. The sky was a malignant white, though it wasn't raining yet.

David opened the door and stood in the dark with her. The horizon to the east was pink-orange with city. He reached for her waist and pulled them hip to hip.

"Remember that first time you accosted me in the dark?" she said.

"A beauty in black."

"I've never been any sort of beauty. You just didn't get the music."

"Are you kidding?" he said. "Did you really think I couldn't fake a review? At twenty-one you can fake anything. No, I followed you out. You really didn't know that?"

"I still don't know it," she said. She almost said, You sounded a little disappointed about the cancer. He'd deny it. He had a way of lying without lying. Once she'd teased him about a trip he and his buddies had taken to Tijuana, at least a year before they'd met. Bet you had some fun, she'd said. I've heard about Tijuana. Well, he'd said, they did. Me, I'm allergic to penicillin.

"You *are* the love of my life," he said.

Emily bent over, away from him. She thought she might be sick. How long had she been a wife? How long had the first light been out? Theirs was another one of those marriages, that was all. Maybe it had always been, but neither knew it until they thought cancer.

"I always thought we had the love of the century." She straightened and laughed.

She heard him swallow. He was sick, too. She thought the words for him: How terribly good to be a grieving widower, alone again, black-haired still, alone again in the night.

"Don't laugh," he said. "Come on, let's go to bed."

"Emmy, Emmy, nothing's changed," he said. "Don't lie there like a stone. Come here. Get with the program."

He'd been afraid to touch her before, when cancer was at work. Now he was still afraid, she thought, his hands on her in a rhythm: nothing's changed, nothing's changed.

But she took him. Thunder sounded like the tympan: bam

bum. The rain bounced on the bedroom window. She thought it must be hail. He moved like one tight, held note and finally, when she was ready to say *breathe, man,* he gave a little glissando moan and slid down.

"You are the love of my life," he said, straight into her ear. "I don't know what I'd have done if you'd really been sick. I couldn't have stood it."

She shifted him off. "I've been giving you a hard time. I've been a basket case."

"I didn't know how to play it. Keep it light and upbeat? Or not work up false hope."

"Well," she said, "we're all right now."

When he began a flutter of snores, she put on her bathrobe and stepped outside. The patio roof kept the heavy rain from her. They would be all right. But her knowledge held steady. Well, so what? she thought. So the light was out, the light that was Emily, the platonic Emily, the primal Emily inside him. So what? They were just married like anybody else. Rain gusted against her bare feet, and she wanted to be cold. She held up her long robe. She wanted a flash flood ripping down the wash below the back yard.

She waited until the rain softened, and then she walked out into the puddles. There was no more program, no story, only a self-pitying, middle-aged woman waiting for some shift in the night's tension. David would laugh at her melodrama. He'd already forgotten the flash when they'd both seen his disappointment that his life wouldn't shift.

Thunder fluttered in the distance like inappropriate applause. She remembered that Mahler had never heard his ninth symphony. She thought she saw David watching through the bedroom window, and she was embarrassed. But inside, from the hallway, she could hear him breathing through his mouth. She rubbed her hair with a towel and put on a pair of socks.

They'd brought in four extra horns when they'd done the Resurrection. The chorus sang: I shall fly away to the light whither no eye pierced. Emily lay on the living room floor. The brown carpet was stiff against her. She thought she could feel the hard earth.

In the pure silence, she saw herself on her metal chair, before her heavy black music stand, and she took her right hand from inside the horn and raised the bell. She played a fire that lit her death, and she looked at it and looked at it. Finally she let out her breath and the stretched fire resolved and disappeared.

Before dawn, Emily awoke on the floor and crawled into bed with her husband. And when she awoke again, the light inhabited her.

The Blood and the Blood and the Blood

HE promised he'd kill me if I left him, and after I found my burgundy maternity dress all sliced up, I believed him. Mama had made me the dress, it had a round lace collar, and when I found it hanging from the light pull in the closet, it looked like one of those fat paper lanterns with the slits in the sides, but all collapsed. I'd worn that dress home from the hospital after Joey, and maybe I looked like I was prego still, but I took the pounds off right away. I couldn't even eat my mother's raised gooey rolls that she brought over to tempt me with, nothing.

"I don't care, you've got to *eat*," Mama told me. "That baby's got to eat." So I ate one and pulled the nuts off a couple others and ate the nuts all crystalled with brown sugar, and drank a coffee cup of milk, but then she left and I threw it up.

So I left and Mama hid me out at her friend's house, that's June who's always been Mama's best friend ever since they had their own babies right next door to each other in those houses in Stoughton Street that aren't there any more, instead there's a row of condominiums. We fixed up a dresser drawer with one of Joey's quilts, the pink one that Richard's sister gave us when Joey was born, and put it on the floor right next to the studio couch in the extra bedroom where I slept. Joey, he'd just lie on his back in the drawer, flailing his arms and legs around like he was trying to grab hold of something but it was invisible and kept jerking just out of his reach.

Richard promised he'd kill me if I left him. At night on June's studio couch I thought of my body with long slits in it, long thin slits from my breasts to my thighs. My collapsed body held the slits together so that the guts couldn't spill out, the heart behind the ribs, but the milk and the blood leaked out and made pink puddles on the closet floor.

June and Mama had been prego together, I don't know how many times I've heard it, and June'd already had Junie and Freddy so she told Mama all about it: how I would be a girl because Mama was carrying me high but June's would be a boy because she was carrying it low and how with Junie her water'd broken in the IGA in the snacks aisle and how the box doc would just stick his rubber fingers in and tell you to quit hollering. That's what I remember June was always telling Timmy: quit your hollering. To me, it was always: quit your barking. I'd had a nervous cough. Mama didn't know anything, I was her first and only and she was nineteen, like me now and here I am with Joey. Once Mama told me that she and June used to play rubber-crutch jokes, and she'd come up with: that's as funny as a Kotex machine in a maternity ward. She'd thought that was so cute. But June had told her there wasn't anything funny about *that*, that there was enough blood in a maternity ward to make Kimberly-Clark billionaires but it was all in nickels. So June had told Mama all about it and finally Mama had told me, so I knew Joey was a boy because I carried him low, which I told Richard's sister but she gave us that pink blanket anyway, and I knew about the armor my muscles would become and the green pain underneath the armor, and I knew about the perfect weight of a diapered baby tucked onto your left arm, and I knew about the blood, too.

So I hid in June's house that she'd moved into after Ernie, that was her husband, died in bed and Freddy had his route moved to Mahomet and he gave her the house. There was just one bedroom, along with the sitting room with the studio couch I was sleeping on. There was a front porch that made me think of the stage in an old school. It was just her by herself now, Ernie dead in bed and Freddy gone to Mahomet and Junie up in Chicago married to a theater owner who had her work the concessions and Timmy, I mean Tim, in the navy on Okinawa, he sent her a pink flowered kimono. But it had never been just her by herself, for years when Timmy and I were kids in the same backyard, there was always some uncle she'd go visit. There's a black-and-white snapshot of me and Timmy in a mostly deflated wading pool and June's in her bathing suit with us, and an Uncle Mack is pouring a sprinkler can over our stringy hair. Our faces are all scrunched up. The Uncle Mack is wearing a suit. I don't know who took the picture.

It was funny, once when Timmy and I were about eleven, we decided to get married. Oh we knew it was play, but we got the Reber twins to get their flower girl dresses on, these pink dotted swiss deals they'd worn in their aunt's wedding, and I got this white slip of Mama's and tied up the shoulder straps, and I got out an old yellowy-white lace tablecloth that some cousins had made for Mama, and draped the thing over my head and let it make the train behind. Timmy gave me a clump of dandelions, which stained Mama's slip but good, but that didn't matter. Here's the thing: we had to sneak into Ernie's room, we never wondered why Mama and Daddy had the same room but Ernie and June had their own, anyway we needed Ernie's vest and a hat for Timmy's groom suit, and Ernie was on a trip, so all we had to do was sneak past June. So of course we slip into the room and it's all dark with the shades down in the afternoon and we pull the door shut behind us and then we turn on the light and of course there's June and the current uncle under the covers. June, she just says, "Now turn that light right back out, Uncle Harry's sick with bad chills and I'm taking care of him. You kids just scram now."

So we scrammed, and Mama gave us Daddy's suit jacket and a cap for Timmy to get married in. "You look funnier than a rubber crutch," she said, and she took our picture in the backyard, I've probably still got that snapshot, those solemn kids, my stained wedding slip puddled around my ankles, I could probably blackmail Timmy who turned out a fairy, at least he told me he thought he was, but June didn't know it.

So when I was fourteen we used to go on hayrides and make out, oh not me and Timmy of course, by then we didn't live next door and just saw each other when we had family deals, anyway I mean me and my group from school. One time I was making out with Glen Mitchell who had whiskers I thought were so sexy when they scratched, and Glen, he puts one hand underneath my sweater, and I say, "Hey," because there's a piece of straw caught on his sleeve and it scratches me, but I guess he thought I said "Hey" so he'd keep his hands to himself. He says, "It's all right, my hands are just cold." He wouldn't have found but a couple of peach pit lumps anyway, but I sat up as if to catch my breath and he had to just let his poor little pinkies take a chill.

But then maybe a few months later, I caught on exactly to the Cold Hands Syndrome, and suddenly I remembered June and the chilled uncle under the covers. I checked it out with Mama, and she admitted that June had had her friends, one and another, for years, and she figured Ernie knew but maybe not. She figured all three kids were Ernie's, they were unmistakably Gilman in the nose which was broad and slightly turned up, Timmy always hated his nose and said it looked like a pig's.

So I and my girlfriends put cold hands and chilled bodies and beds and fathers and babies together. And later on there came Richard who had no chills, oh no, but enough heat to steam the windows of his Maverick but thoroughly, shades might as well have been pulled around that back seat. It's sickening now, but he drew a heart on the condensation, and maybe I myself assisted in the window-steaming. And of course I came to know of *that* blood, and of course we got married as soon as we graduated. Even we didn't know if we had to, Joey was just exactly the right time afterward. Timmy, excuse me, Tim, he asked me before the wedding if I was carrying Richard's child, that's the way he said it, carrying Richard's child, and I said maybe, I didn't really know, but there had been that steamed-up back seat of the Maverick and one of my knees in the air and the other leg hanging over the seat and the richness of that air was like breathing in a sickroom with the vaporizer going and that blood—oh, I didn't say that but anyway I al*lud*ed to it. And that's when Tim told me he thought he had to be a fairy but not to tell anyone.

So now here I was in June's extra room with my baby in a drawer on the floor, waiting for Richard to find me and kill me like he said and I believed him.

I picked Joey up and leaned against the studio couch cushions that I'd take off later to make it into a bed, I picked him up though he wasn't even crying, and little beggar that he was, he turned his head for my breasts. *Little beggar, little Joey, Joey, pulling me into you.* I thought of transfusions and blood easing along a clear tube, body to body.

"Look at the little beggar's nose," Richard had said. "Look at those nostrils, will you? You know what that schnoz will look like, he gets bigger? I'll tell you: a pig's nose."

It was a baby's nose, that was all, a baby's nose which was mostly no nose at all. And I might be transfusing him with my body's milk, but inside his intact little body was waiting nothing but human blood and heart unprotected by ribs, vessels tangled incurably.

"Listen, girl," June said at the door, "your mama's coming to get you."

"You can come in," I said. I hated to have her see me nursing Joey, she'd always had such huge buzooms that she had permanent half-inch dents in her shoulders from her bra straps trying to hold them up, and here I was with these pointy little things that even the milk wasn't doing much for. But Richard always liked them or he didn't know any better, just like Joey—they both just latched right on.

"Your mom's got this shopping bug," June said. She was wearing purple pants and a pink-purple-orange flowered blouse, it sounds worse than it looked. "She says you and Joey don't have but a couple changes of clothes and she's going to fix you both up." She shook her head, and the curlers bounced. They were the pink foam kind I and my friends used to wear in junior high, and the dog would eat them and leave pink-swirled deposits on the snow in winter and in spring there'd be all these curly pink curlers on the dead wet grass. "Me," she said, "I just know your mama's hooked on baby clothes. Just like me." It was true: she had five big baby dolls in the house, she'd bought them for herself except for one Junie'd got her, and she kept buying real baby outfits for them and changing their clothes and setting them in corners. It was true: we'd all loved babies, June'd had three and here I was with Joey at nineteen, and Mama'd have had more if she could have but after me they'd tied her off. I don't know why.

June was to watch Joey, and Mama came to pick me up, and we went to the Holiday Hills, why they named it that I can't figure, in the middle of the cornfields, and we had supper at the pizza place there. Mama loved pizza now that Daddy had died, she'd never had it before because he thought it was slumber party food, and we even each had a beer. She bought me a fall outfit, all green and rust, and Joey a terry suit and a little blue deal with ducks that said Grandma Loves Me.

So then some lady's baby lets out a squall in Penney's and all of a sudden my blouse is soaked with milk, I don't know how my body knows it ought to start giving forth when a baby cries, anybody's baby. My baby, Richard's baby, Mama's baby, June's baby, Timmy's baby, it doesn't matter, baby cries, milk runs.

So Mama takes me back to June's and we just use my key that June gave me and open the door, and there's June and somebody lying on the floor and they've got my baby between them. And I grab Joey and run back into my sitting room. I hear talking and then Mama comes in and says, "Judge not lest ye be," and kisses Joey and kisses me and leaves.

At night I keep Joey up on the studio couch with me, even though I've heard of mothers rolling over and suffocating their babies in their sleep, but I can't put him in that drawer. I dream and dream of my body with long vertical slits in it from breasts to thighs, my body judged and carved, hanging from a light pull.

In the morning, June brings me a cup of coffee sweetened with cocoa, and she says, "Listen, that was just Timmy's Uncle Jack and we were just playing with Joey on the floor, he'd been fussing, so don't you think anything, girl."

And I took the coffee and said, "Don't mind me, I don't think a thing," very primly.

So then Timmy, I mean Tim, he calls from the bus station, and June goes to get him. It's pure daylight and I stay there by myself, Richard doesn't know where June lives, and I'm not afraid except I am. I call Mama and we talk about how cute Joey looks in the new terry suit and she says I ought to put the Grandma-Loves-Me duck suit on one of June's dolls for a surprise joke. I ask her if Daddy was ever jealous and thought maybe I wasn't his own child, and she says, "No, not your daddy, never, ever, not your daddy. Now Ernie, that's something else, but I don't even think Ernie ever did think a thing."

"Sometimes," I say, "I don't think it matters much anyway, you've got this baby on your arm."

And Mama says: "What are you saying? Of course it matters, are you trying to tell me something?"

So I start crying like some lady at her time of month, like Mama—"Don't mind me, it's a week before my period, I just can't help it." I couldn't believe she'd say that in front of Daddy, but I guess the blood and the blood and the blood explain it all right, and I guess I might even have said it to Richard if we'd been all right and he hadn't said he'd kill me if I left him and if I hadn't left him.

So June comes in with Tim, oh my old friend Timmy, and I can't help it, I hug him and hold him, he's all navy filled out, and I want us to be kids playing dress-up, skinny kids in a wading pool in the backyard, not in uniforms, not with babies crying in drawers in closed rooms.

"Raw fish," he says, "I been eating raw fish and look what it's done." June goes for Joey and Timmy says quickly, "I was wrong, you know," and I know right off what he means.

Timmy is saying, "You sit on this tatami floor," and the front door is opening, and June is holding Joey out for me, and the milk is leaking all over my blouse again, and Richard is there in the living room where June and Uncle Jack had been lying with my baby, Richard's baby, between them the night before, and I'm reaching for Joey.

So Richard shoots June in the knee and then he looks at me as she falls back down to the floor, as if to say he meant me, or he didn't mean me but what we all might have done, it hardly mattered but someone had to be shot. He slammed the front door and he was gone.

There's nothing to the rest. Timmy called the ambulance and Mama went to stay with June in the hospital, and Timmy drove me and Joey around and around until we knew he wasn't after us and left us at the Sleep-Eze out on 120. He went to *his* mama and I nursed Joey and turned on the TV and tried to think of all my years without Richard, all my years coiling through my own body like blood, all my years as tangled as anyone's.

High Country

EVERY fall, up from the desert, Clemmie and Leah camped another five hundred feet higher. This year they met at nine thousand feet, each with her dog. The previous year they'd gotten drunk on margaritas at night and made an extravagant fire and cried about dogs dead or dying. Leah's Bud, an ancient terrier-something that smelled bad and looked, Clemmie thought, like a burnt meatloaf, was the remains of a long-dead marriage to a press operator who had died of cirrhosis long after he'd left Leah and Budweiser. The puppy had been a birthday present to him nineteen years ago. Last fall, Leah had cried for the dying Bud—Clemmie remembered her coarse face, ochreous in the light of the fire, smoothed by tears—but here was Bud, still alive, on yet another final camping trip. Last year, Clemmie's own grief had been raw, with the white shepherd, who'd been her son's dog until he left for college, dead only two weeks. After the dog had been buried, her son asked her to send some tufts of fur for memory's sake, and she'd finally found some she hadn't vacuumed up under the bed. This year Mark had again let her bring his dog, Bandit, a young husky who was sweet at home but antisocial otherwise.

Leah was sitting on top of her Mazda drinking a beer when Clemmie pulled into the campground. "I just got here, too," she said. "What do you think? We've got the place to ourselves."

The sites had picnic tables and fire rings and shared a pair of outhouses. It wasn't primitive camping, as it was with her own family, but they were above the aspens, high into pine forest, high and away from the scramble of life below.

"Looks good," Clemmie said. "In fact, it looks positively great.

I was thinking on the way up here—two more years of this and we'll be at the summit. What'll we do then?"

"Maybe my mother'll be croaked. Maybe you'll have left Mark. In two years, who the fuck knows. In two years we may be ready for that big campground in the sky."

Clemmie opened the hatchback and Bandit leapt out, ran in furious circles, and then squatted.

"I don't know why you'd say that," she said. But Leah, on the far side of her car pulling out gear, didn't answer. Clemmie watched her unload lawn chairs, a new tent, canopy, propane lantern, cot, giant cooler, the works. Bud watched, too, if Bud could even see, from his brown pillow.

"I can't believe you got all that into your car," Clemmie said. "We could stay up here a month."

"I could go for that. God, you don't know the half of it. Did I tell you what my mother did now? She brushed her teeth with lipstick. Came out with her mouth all red—scared the shit out of me."

Clemmie laughed. "Sorry. It isn't funny, I know that." She scuffed leaves and rocks away from a flat patch of ground. Her own mother, dead of cancer years before, used to take her and her sister to a Lake Michigan campground, before they hit puberty and turned on her. They rented a camper, with pull-out beds and built-in sink and icebox, and left their father behind. He, after all, had grown up on a farm with no indoor plumbing. In her memory, it always rained on those trips, and the three of them sat in the camper and played Yahtzee. She would say she needed to go to the outhouse so she'd have an excuse to run outside in her bathing suit. She remembered the cold muddy feel of the wet sand and, when her bare feet broke through, the warm fluffy sand underneath. She ran like a little animal beside the gray booming lake, beneath the sky so low and flat and gray she might be flying. In the camper, her mother undid her braids so her hair would dry, and they ate greasy potato chips and peanut butter sandwiches. Sometimes, still, her mother's absence knocked the wind out of her. She pictured Leah playing cards with her mother, safe in her compact house. But she didn't know if she'd have her mother back at any price.

"Laugh," Leah said. "*I* do. You have to. I hear her in the middle of the night and get up and there she is, back in bed but all dressed up, girdle and red dress and heels and all. You have to laugh. The funny thing is, she used to be so hard to please. I could never do anything right. Now she's just as sweet as you'd like." She took two beers from the cooler. "I don't know about you, but I need this. And I don't mean just another cold one. Hey, listen, I bought a new tent, and it's plenty big for both of us."

"Oh, well, I don't know. Maybe I'll just put up our little tent. You and Budweiser don't need my big hulking dog all over the place at night." She and Mark had bought the orange pup tent at Kmart for their honeymoon in Florida. She shook it out, still in one piece after years of camping with their son and dogs.

"Okay, suit yourself," Leah said.

Clemmie didn't even know why she wanted to sleep alone in her own little family tent. One thing about Leah, though: she might have hurt feelings for a moment, but she didn't sweat the small stuff. Or hold grudges. Before she'd even married Owen, she'd had her tubes tied, and said she'd never been sorry, and here she was now with a mother turned child.

They made their camp like little girls playing house, with that same pleasure of arranging an imitation grown-up life. When Leah put a neon-striped dog sweater on Budweiser, Clemmie thought that their dogs were their dolls, which had been, of course, imitation children. When she camped with her husband and son, their real life disappeared. She carried an image of Mark and a long-haired Drew in tan canvas hunting jackets, laughing and trying to skin a rabbit with the half-grown white shepherd jumping for it. On the women's camping trips, they left their real lives behind, but from the high country they looked down and observed the little characters and worked over the old stories.

Mid-afternoon, they left Bud like a stuffed dog on his pillow and hiked to Eagle Rock with Bandit. They tramped up the switchbacking trail, silent, arms swinging. Bandit ran ahead and stopped until they caught up and then charged up the trail. Striding along, clean and strong, out of her grown-up life, Clemmie was struck by a thought, as suddenly as if a pine branch had caught her in the face: she *could* leave Mark. She had never considered that, not really. Her cheeks stung and her eyes watered.

"Did I tell you about the pantyliners?" Leah said. "My mother was using pantyliners because she has a tendency to dribble. At first the only problem was she'd forget to change them. Or her underwear, either. Then I discovered she was wearing them in her shoes."

Clemmie laughed so hard she had to sit on a boulder. "Oh god. What a picture. You're making *me* dribble."

"Yeah but that's not all. Next she's putting them in her bra."

"I hope you warned the sitter. It has to be strange, taking care of your own mother like a child. Like when Drew was little, changing his pants, bathing him, getting up at night, following him around so he wouldn't hurt himself."

"Yeah, but at least you had a husband to help. This is the first real breather I've had in months."

"I don't think Mark did much to help. It's hard to remember."

"The other thing is, you know a kid's going to grow up. It's the reverse with my mother. She's going backwards. Pretty soon she'll be a falling-down toddler and then an infant messing her diapers, and then what?" Leah laughed and choked. "I'll have to take her into the womb."

The baby had been born with a good head of dark hair, like Mark's, but when he was six months old it turned fine and reddish. She remembered the baby crawling across the living room. She remembered that wild red hair. She squinted. She'd been trying to teach him not to pull on the lamp cord. When she put him down he took off on all fours straight for the cord. She slapped his wrist with two fingers. Every time he grabbed the cord she slapped, until his wrist was red. Finally she gave up on the lesson and moved the lamp, and for years, whenever he needed directing, she'd see that soft white wrist with her finger stripes on it. Drew's baby hair had turned again, from red to blond like hers. Only recently, since he'd been away at school, had it darkened.

"I'd tell my mother to take a shower," Leah said, "and she'd get in with her clothes on. And leave the shower curtain outside the tub, to boot. Now I just get in with her. I soap her whole body down and wash her hair."

From the bare saddle of Eagle Rock they could see waves of color below—dusty green to red to heated yellow—as if the seasons were climbing the mountains. Here above timberline, winter, pale green lichen fed on rocks and the late afternoon light was flat.

The loop, they decided, would get them back to camp at dusk, and so they took the same trail down. Bandit panted behind them. They lost footing sometimes in the loose red earth and pine needles, and Clemmie's knees tightened in the effort to slow descent.

For a moment, back at camp, they couldn't find Budweiser. They checked the big dome tent and looked behind the coolers. "He never leaves that pillow," Leah said. "But I can't believe anybody'd take him. Let's face it, he is not prime dog flesh."

Then they heard Bandit snarl, and there was Bud doddering over to his water bowl, as if he had rachet wheels for hip joints.

"Bandit, no," Clemmie said. "No, no, no. No snarling. You leave Budweiser alone. Look, you have your own water."

"Oh they're okay," Leah said. "You get too worked up." She picked up the little dog and carried him over to Bandit. "You two can be buddies. In fact, it's a good thing you're as tall as you are," she said to Bandit, "or the old man here'd be trying to put it to you. He's not dead yet. He's been known to work on his pillow if he can't find anything else."

Bandit's black lips were back. "Let's just let them ignore each other," Clemmie said.

"This little old dog is just like me," Leah said. "I haven't been laid in years either. I can't even hump a pillow."

Clemmie liked the loud coarseness. Beside Leah, she was reassuringly prim.

"There is that advantage to being married," she said. In bed, though, Mark bit her neck or her earlobe. Even as she was ascending into pleasure, she was shrinking away from his teeth. "I'm going to pick up some firewood."

"Well, I'm going to make Bloody Marys."

As they laid a fire and set up the grill, drank Bloody Marys and fed their dogs, well apart, the ground held its light in the pine branches. The light bled into the dark blue straight above, so at dusk the sky was cloth and they were inside a huge tent, and then the earth absorbed all the light and they were in deep night. They ate the chicken and the corn Leah had brought, poured wine into

Clemmie and Mark's tin camp cups, rinsed and wiped their toy dishes, ate molten marshmallows from sticks, bits of bark included.

"Let's not get onto dead dogs this time," Leah said.

"No," Clemmie said. "But I still miss that old dog. That one was the dog of my life. You think when you're a kid *that* dog is the only dog that'll really count. Of course, she was really Drew's dog. But when he went to Boston, we said she was mine and Bandit was Mark's."

"Bandit looks like your dog to me. Could have fooled me."

Clemmie stroked the insides of the dog's pliable ears, and Bandit leaned into the pleasure. "She is mine. But I don't think Mark knows it. He's so rough with her. It's all in play. He never punishes her or anything. When he reaches out to pet her, she cringes and goes belly-up, as if he's going to hit her."

"Submissive. He's the heap big alpha male."

"You got it." Clemmie laughed and shivered. "You should see him, down on his hands and knees, growling at her. He kind of raises up on his knuckles like the lord of the gorillas."

"I saw this movie once with the woman tied to the bed and the man whipping her. Some people get off on that submission business."

Clemmie put on her sweatshirt and filled their tin cups. Leah, she thought, was her usual blunt self out here, but a fire on a dark mountain—and the alcohol, that contributed—would open those who held their thoughts close, like secrets, secrets or shame. "Only in the movies," she said. "So what're you doing watching pornographic movies, anyway?"

"Long time ago. With Owen at some old theater. You know what?" She laughed. "It was really, really boring."

"What did Owen think?"

"Men are different. Owen loved it. As soon as we got home—well, anyway. What do you think, if they made a pornographic movie for dogs, you think they'd watch it?"

"Don't. That's obscene. That's like imagining your parents doing it. Or your children."

"Let me tell you a secret, my dear innocent Clementine. Everybody's a sexual creature. Your grown-up son. My mother. Though if she gets a twinge, she forgets it before she can do anything about it."

"This from the woman who hasn't done it in years. But it's not exactly sexual, I don't think. It's not lust. It's *touch*."

"Right. This from the woman who can't stand to be touched."

It was true, Clemmie thought, but she hadn't known that Leah or anybody else saw that she pulled away from the casual hug, the conversational hand on her arm. "I'm not that way with Mark, though," she said. "That's different."

"Poor old Bud's shaking. I'm going to put him to bed. You pour."

Clemmie added wood to the fire, dropping it to make sparks burst up. "I'm getting drunk," she said. She filled the tin cups again.

Leah crawled out of her tent, though it was high enough for her to stand inside. "There. All tucked in."

"Watch this." Clemmie dropped a branch onto the fire and laughed at the rush of sparks.

Leah settled into the lawn chair on her side of the fire. She pulled a beach towel around her shoulders. "That little dog is the only thing I have left from Owen," she said. "I was just thinking of that. Not that I wanted anything. He left me for that woman he lived with until he died. I didn't want a goddamn thing from him. The worst of it was, it didn't even occur to him to take Bud. *His* dog."

She was crying, Clemmie thought, although Leah was such a defiant head-up crier, it was hard to tell through the smoke and fire. She'd heard the story of Owen before. She didn't remind Leah that he hadn't been the only one carrying on with someone else when he left.

"He didn't even for a flash of a second consider taking his dog. Not for a splinter of an instant. I was just as glad when he moved out. Took his stereo. But not his dog. I didn't miss him. Sometimes I can't believe how lonely it gets, though."

"You have your mother, anyway. I wish I had my mother."

"I don't have my mother. At first, when she moved in, I had her. I even had a real mother, not the rough woman I had to grow up with. I used to think my ass had permanent hand prints." She hunched into her beach towel and poked the fire until the stick flamed. "She turned nice for a while, but then she disappeared. You can't talk to her now. Or you can say anything. You could say, 'Mother you stinking heap of dogshit you,' and she'd smile and say, 'Isn't that nice.'"

Clemmie and Mark had been to Leah's for dinner a month ago. Leah asked her mother to hand her the serving spoon she'd put on her own plate. Her mother tried to hand over her knife. No, Mother, Leah said patiently. The spoon. The old woman picked up a lettuce leaf and held it out and then tried a pat of butter. Finally Leah just reached over and retrieved the serving spoon. Jesus, Mark said on their way home, she didn't know what a spoon was. Shoot me if I ever get that way. I mean it. Put me out of your misery. What Clemmie remembered was how hard the woman had tried to please, how desperately she'd smiled.

"I picked her up at day care the other day, though, and she knew me," Leah said. "She yelled Lee-lee and came running over and hugged me. She gets this sly grin on her face and takes this box from behind her back. They do these projects. She's made me a box out of popsicle sticks glued together and varnished. It's got my name on the top, in glitter."

"That's enough to break your heart." Clemmie's mother had died years ago, and her son had flown across the country, and the white shepherd was gone. If she left Mark, everybody would have left everybody. Except she'd keep Bandit. Mark would put up a fight, but she'd keep her dog. "Our fire's leaving us," she said. "I'm freezing." She kicked the unburned ends of sticks into the throbbing coals and they flared.

"Hey, didn't your mother ever tell you not to play with fire? What are you, drunk?" Leah said. "Shitfire, I'm drunk too."

"Shit fire and save matches. That's what Mark says."

"Did he ever hurt you? A couple times I wondered."

"Mark? You mean hit me? Oh no. No, never. I wouldn't have stayed with him. I promise you that." A coal of shame beat inside her.

"I'm freezing, too." Leah curled up on the lawn chair. "Sometimes I feel like I don't have a friend in the world."

"You've got me. I'm your friend. And others, I'm sure. You've got a ton of friends."

"If I needed help, nobody'd help me."

"Well sure they would. I'd help you. You'd only have to say the word." As long as the word isn't spoon, she thought, and tried to hold her face straight.

"Would you help me, Clemmie?"

"Of course I would."

"Help me, Clemmie." Leah reached her arm out from the beach towel.

"I would," she insisted. "I would."

She pictured what they'd look like from above, two small women in separate aluminum chairs. But she couldn't move from her side of the collapsed fire. The wood was pale with ashes.

In her sleeping bag, with Bandit beside her, Clemmie thought Leah would forget that she'd been left alone by the remains of the fire. Mark hadn't abused her, that was certain, or their son either. He'd been a little rough with the boy, but that had been playing, wrestling and chasing each other. Rough-housing. He'd never seen the flicker of desperation in Drew's eyes as he ran. If Drew or Clemmie pulled back, Mark said, Oh now, that didn't hurt you, and left them alone in disgust.

He used to spank Drew, though. Mark believed kids needed a good swat on the behind to teach them. The last time he'd spanked Drew, the terrible time, the boy was thirteen. Clemmie didn't remember what he'd done to be spanked. But she'd seen from the kitchen. Drew was fighting back, twisting, arms flying. And Mark had gone wild, pounding on the boy. And Clemmie, fixing supper in the kitchen, had stood stock still and then someone yelled or all of them were yelling and crying and Mark grabbed the boy up in a ferocious hug.

The wind rattled the nylon tent, and for an instant Clemmie thought it was raining. The boy was hers the way the dogs were. It was she he called now from Boston, during the day when his dad wouldn't be home. They'd joked privately about Mark. Drew called him the Home Despot. But it was with affection, Clemmie thought. For years she'd been a bit awkward with her son, trying not to be the opposite parent, not so eager to please that she'd hand him lettuce leaves if she couldn't give what he wanted. And at the heart of it all, like her own solitary body in this tent in this wide night, at the heart was her shame. She had not protected him.

★

In the morning they drank coffee and moaned and washed in cold water. The weeds were rimed with frost, and Clemmie pulled up her hood. She chattered to cover up Leah's silence, whether from embarrassment or hangover or hurt she didn't know. They had two more days on the mountain together.

"You want some breakfast?" Clemmie said. "I'll cook."

"No, I'm just going to have a granola bar."

"You want to take a hike? It'd warm us up."

"Oh, why not." Leah stretched. "Remind me to skip the Bloody Marys tonight."

Clemmie was relieved. Leah didn't hold a grudge, and maybe she didn't remember she had one to hold. "You do make a mean Bloody Mary," she said. She flung her arms wide in the steamy cold morning. She had wakened during the night to the wind that sounded like rain, and she'd breathed in the cold clean air. She'd thought of Mark in their bed, warm in the heated room but with only himself to touch. She'd turned over in the sleeping bag, sighing with cold pleasure, postponing the idea of leaving Mark until the daylight.

Leah opened a can of Mighty Dog for Budweiser.

"Oh good idea," Clemmie said. "I'll feed Bandit, too, before we take off."

Leah carried Bud out of the tent. He was still wearing his neon-striped sweater. She set his bowl down before him. "Be right back," she said. "I'm going to the powder room."

Clemmie bent to her supply box for the bag of dry dog food. After, she knew it was her fault for not paying attention.

She heard the threat and the snarl of her big dog and then the single yelp of the little old dog. She was up and yelling, "No Bandit, no Bandit," but Bandit was wolfing Bud's food and Bud was rolling over and over down the slope to the cold fire ring. He hit one of the stones and stopped. Leah came running to him, pulling up her jeans.

Shaking, Clemmie tied Bandit to a tree. She was sick with the spurt of adrenaline. "I'm sorry, I'm sorry," she said. "I don't think she bit him. She just wanted his food. Did she bite him, do you think? I think she just scared him. Can he get up?"

High Country

Budweiser lay still in his sweater. When Leah tried to pick him up, he snapped at her.

"Oh I'm sorry," Clemmie said again. "Please, please, little guy, you'll be all right. We'll just let you lie here for a couple minutes. Did that big mean dog scare you?" She heard her own sick voice and shut up. She left Leah sitting on the ground beside Bud.

After a few minutes, Leah called her. "Look, he's up. If he's walking around, he can't have any broken bones, can he? He's let me check him over and I can't feel anything."

Clemmie crouched beside Leah and the staggering dog. "I'll never forgive myself," she whispered.

"She's just a dog, acting like a dog. You can't blame her."

"It's myself I blame. I should have been paying attention." She turned to look at Bandit who was as flat to the ground as she could make herself.

Leah said, "Don't be so hard on yourself. But listen, I don't want to go hiking right now. I just want to sit here with him."

"I'll leave you alone. I'll get my mutt out of here for a while." Clemmie and Bandit sidled away from camp and walked morosely out of the pines and around a pathless high meadow. The high peaks were lit but the red and yellow groundcover was muted by shadow. The fog smoked away. At the lower curve was a stand of aspen, and Clemmie headed for the long naked trunks with their flares of yellow held high. Closer, though, she called the dog and turned back. The aspens had eyes scattered up the pale gray boles.

When they returned, Leah was gone. Her tent was collapsed, and she'd taken all her other gear. She must have cleared out in a hurry, Clemmie thought. She hadn't bothered with the ball of foil in the ashes or a rag of tissue caught in the weeds. Clemmie imagined there'd be blood on the tent floor, soaking through the nylon and blackening the earth underneath.

The note, held down with a rock on the tent, read: *Sorry. I'm going back. I want to get Budweiser to the vet. Bring my tent? Extra chicken and salad in your cooler. You should stay up here. This is nobody's fault. He's a very old dog. Call you in a couple days. L.*

After she folded Leah's tent and packed it in its stuff sack, Clemmie heated more water and drank cappuccino made from powdered mix. She sat on the ground and read with the dog against her leg. She waited for the guilt to subside. Leah didn't blame her. But she'd have been angry, herself, at anyone who allowed her dog to be hurt. Think about it, she told herself, half asleep on the ground in the warming morning. You're the one who allowed him to do the hurting. If hurting it was.

She drifted through the afternoon, letting the high country wash her out. The fall wind carried the smell of pine resin and faraway rain. She wasn't thinking at all, but as she hiked up a trail and down, as she made supper and built a modest fire, her limbs loosened. It had been a tight life, holding herself back from Mark.

She zipped herself and Bandit into the tent just after dark and read by flashlight. She pictured how the tent would look from above: a soft beating light in an orange skin. She could hardly believe all of them, father and son and mother and two big dogs, had shared this very tent. But they had, they had year after year, they had slept in this space together. Then Mark could touch them all, and they hadn't cringed or been hurt, either.

She imagined Drew, her well grown-up son, studying at a brown desk, the talisman of white dog hair in his jeans pocket. He'd carefully transfer it to a little box at night and to his clean pair of jeans in the morning, and set out into the wide snowy city, knowing he was protected.

She woke into the dark when the rainy wind hit the tent, and she unzipped the flap and wiggled out of her sleeping bag enough to stick her head out. It wasn't raining. Inside, when the wind rattled the nylon again, she put her hands on the tent to meet his fierce touch.

Little Egypt

THEY'D never seen the baby but the first thing they said when Suzanne and Gary pulled up was, "Dexter Donald killed hisself."

In the brown yard, Suzanne could smell the septic tank.

Francine Grace Potter hugged her son. Then she hugged Suzanne and felt the baby between their thin bodies. "Oh my," she said. "You didn't lie to me, did you? Olin, will you look at this? They've got theirselves a baby." She led them across the brown yard and into the house, leaving the baby wrapped and uninspected.

"How'd he do it?" Gary asked.

"Who's Dexter Donald?" Suzanne said. She sat on the brown couch and carefully unwound the yellow blanket, though she wanted to unveil the baby with a flourish.

"Shot hisself," her father-in-law said.

Francine Grace stepped cautiously toward the baby.

"Well, you don't have to be afraid, Mom," Gary said. "She's not exactly a freak."

"Herbert Gary!" she said. "Remember you're speaking to your own mother that loves you." She held her arms out for the baby.

"You know Dexter Donald had them two little boys."

"Who's Dexter Donald, anyway?" Suzanne said.

"She's just a little browner than the rest of us," Gary said.

All the way down from Chicago, Suzanne had known something was wrong. "Nothing is wrong," Gary had said patiently. After five years, she knew him well enough to keep quiet. The carseat between them kept her to the passenger's side. The baby slept and Suzanne watched the flat land coast by. The afternoon was muted by the fall haze of southern Illinois. She watched the fields,

79

Meg Files

stubbly brown or fuzzed with the pale gray-green of winter wheat. She slid the cassette of Beethoven's Violin Concerto into the tape deck. Patches of woods slid by; the trees still held their leaves, the rust and muted yellow leaching into the brown. "Did you know that Tchaikovsky, not Beethoven, wrote the cadenza in this recording?" she asked. She saw a diner named Pharaoh's Cafe. The next ancient little town had a Phoenix Cleaners. She was befogged by the music and the gray-blue clouds. This was the way she must absorb Gary's moody silence, she thought, and she felt aphonic and pure, like a horn with a mute in the bell, choked with the man's complexity and the sleeping energy of the baby. She rode south to Gary's home, watching the bulky watercolor sky.

"Guess what we named her," Suzanne said. She lifted the baby to her mother-in-law.

"You got her from where, did you say?" her father-in-law said.

"You say you named this sweetheart after her grandma?" Francine Grace said, joking. "Aww, you shouldn't have."

Gary had thought she'd want to name the baby after her own dead mother, but she couldn't bear to think of a reincarnated Kathryn. When her mother died, she hardly wanted a child any more, and all the way across the Pacific she was afraid she'd prodded Gary into the adoption, and filled out the forms, and paid the money, and told the caseworker about their love of children and their barren sex life, and painted a secondhand crib, all for her mother. Until her mother died, she hadn't known that her need wasn't as much for a child as for the excited discussion of babies and nurseries and reminiscence with her mother. "We don't know for sure yet," she'd told her mother a month before she died, "but we think we're getting a baby from the Philippines."

"I won't start shopping yet," her mother had said. "But as soon as you get the word, just watch my smoke." She hadn't waited for the word, though, and when Suzanne emptied her mother's apartment, she found a drawer full of new baby clothes.

"I used to babysit Dexter Donald," Francine Grace said. "His mother would have to be at the factory early, and Dexter Donald would be over here for breakfast and then after school. Every blessed day."

"We named her Sara," Suzanne said. "Sara Grace."

"Old Bucky," Gary said. "We always called him Bucky. And not because his last name was Buchanan, like you'd think. 'They call me Bucky Beaver 'cause I fim fo good,' " he said, making buck teeth.

"She's a sweetie," Francine Grace said, holding the baby out to examine her. "Is she a schweetheart? Is she Grandma's schweet 'ittle Sara Grace?" She lifted the baby above her head and shook her gently.

The baby spit up on Francine Grace's upturned face.

Suzanne's mother had raised her in the city. She humored Gary when he remembered his boyhood of long dirt roads and Robin Hood woods and one-tangerine Christmases, but she didn't understand. She'd have liked to have a dog, that was all: otherwise the Chicago apartment was her right home. She remembered her mother's gloved hand holding hers just before she was given over to the crossing guard at the corner. She remembered that her mother slept with her own mother's silk glove under her pillow. She had sat on the toilet-seat lid and watched her mother put on her face; she'd handed her mother one square of toilet paper to blot her lipstick on and then held the red-kissed tissue over the wastebasket. She remembered that drifting scrap, blown by the heat of the register, her mother's kiss sailing the currents. Now she was an orphan, she thought. Now she was just like the baby.

"Clarence said he used that single-barreled 20-gauge," Olin said. "Put it in his mouth." He shook his head.

"Christ," Gary said.

"Done it with them little boys right there," Francine Grace said. "That's what Mamie Floyd told Emmadine. His wife was over at Mount Vernon at that big new mall. Her girlfriends dropped her off and Kate, she opened the kitchen door and there was them little boys just sitting on the floor all blood-splattered."

Suzanne pictured a pretty, dark-haired girl hollering *See y'all* to her friends in a station wagon, laughing, fighting the back door with her arms full of shopping bags and shoeboxes, saying, *Lookit this, Dexter Donald* . . . or would she called him *Bucky* . . . or *Honey.*

The baby was crying, a dainty, well-mannered cry. She was a mild baby. Suzanne wished she could slip into the bedroom where she and Gary would sleep and unbutton her blouse for the baby.

But everyone knew the baby was a Filipina orphan. "Honey, would you get the bottle from the diaper bag?" she said.

She'd flown over the Pacific alone to claim the baby. Gary couldn't leave the office. His job wasn't all that secure as it was, he'd said, what with the new management. He'd humored her need for a child, willing, she thought, only to please her, exaggerating his enthusiasm for the caseworker. He wasn't *un*willing, anyway, he told Suzanne. She already had the papers, her passport, and the tickets when her mother died. What would happen to the potential energy that had been summoned if she changed her mind? Alone in Manila, she'd seen the child prostitutes and the street children, six-year-olds carrying one-year-olds back to packing-crate shelters. When she'd found the agency office and waited on an orange plastic couch for an hour, she told herself she was performing a rescue. When Carmen Diaz, with whom she'd been collaborating across the ocean for a year, walked in and handed her the baby, she thought first of the description she'd give her mother. Nervously she'd carried the baby onto the plane. But she'd been such a good baby, sleeping and taking the bottle and burping on the schedule Carmen Diaz had written out, and she'd been so admired by the stewardesses, a porcelain child in a pink dress, that Suzanne had begun to see the three of them as a family. She saw untaken snapshots: mother-father-baby-makes-three arrangements against the painted brick wall of their apartment, with the chrome-framed posters taken down to make a white background.

Holding the bottle for the baby doll in her mother-in-law's kitchen, Suzanne said, "Nobody'll tell me who Dexter Donald was."

"He's just somebody who lived down the road from us," Gary told her patiently.

"Just somebody!" Francine Grace said. "Just somebody who practically lived here, I guess. Just somebody I packed around like I packed you, Herbert Gary."

"Dad, can I talk to you?" Gary said.

"Come on," Olin said. "I need me some help with them dog pens."

When they'd gone, Francine Grace raised her eyebrows inquiringly at Suzanne. Her own mother would have done the same. "I don't know what's bothering him," she said. "He's your son."

Little Egypt

★

The small white frame church sat beside the dirt road, with weed fields in front and in back, sat still like a mangy cat hopelessly watching a cricket. Though it was only a quarter mile from the Potters' house, they drove, parking beside the church among the brown live oaks.

Inside, a starched fat man whispered, "Good to have you here, Potts, Francine Grace. And Herbert Gary, you home for a while this time?"

They walked the thin green carpet to the closed coffin. It was dark gray with a pattern of twisting vines encircling it. *Gun-metal gray*, Suzanne thought, looking for warped shotguns and limp arms worked into the vines. The coffin lay on a long table, the kind of table kept folded in the basement until the next covered-dish dinner.

She held the baby close with a corner of the receiving blanket over her face. She wondered if the Potters would want to have the baby baptized in their church or not. They turned away from the coffin, and Suzanne thought, *The Potters: You're a Potter, too, girl*. She glanced at the front row where the widow sat straight beside an old man in overalls and a black coat. Dexter Donald's little boys were absent. Kate Buchanan was not the pretty, dark-haired girl Suzanne had imagined, but a thick, saucer-faced woman with teased hair.

Suzanne followed the Potters and Gary to the next-to-last pew. She counted the pews: eleven on each side of the single aisle. Beside the coffin, on either side of a blond pulpit, stood an American flag and a white flag with a red cross. The chancel was nothing but one step up, more thin green carpet, two pairs of short pews facing each other, a portable pulpit, and an upright piano. She thought of the grand church of her mother's funeral, the abstract glory in the stained glass windows high into the clerestory, the pipe organ playing the "Ode to Joy"—the Christian version, but close enough. It was bathetic to look for the elements of the cruciform church in this little box, she thought. She settled in beside her mother-in-law. This was only Dexter Donald Buchanan's service. Her mother had been lofted from the church to Mt. Hope Mausoleum, slid in next to her long-dead husband. She was not here.

A lumpy woman with a beehive hairdo approached the piano where a thin-faced woman already sat. "We'll do number thirty-seven," she announced, and the piano introduced a few bars. The congregation of two dozen stood and sang "Rock of Ages." Suzanne held the sleeping baby and looked on with Francine Grace. *Cleft for me.* What rock would ever be cleft for her? She thought of her own rock body fissuring; she thought of a shrunken Gary and a miniature baby crawling into the rifts.

The starched fat man who'd greeted them at the door stood at the pulpit. "I'm going to just say a little bit about Dexter Donald," he said. "Preacher Wilkins, he disallowed any preaching on account of, uh, on account of the manner of Dexter Donald's demise. But we all knew him and we're mourning right along with Katie. He was a good man. Only when he got boozed up . . . sorry, Katie, but everybody knows he was getting boozed up, packing them bottles. Packing them troubles. Ain't none of us could've done a thing, so I don't want Katie nor any of you thinking *if only this, that, or the other thing.* Now I believe in my heart how Dexter Donald's troubles are being right now packed around by Jesus, amen."

The woman with the beehive hairdo led two more hymns, singing on key in a whining voice, moving from note to note with a sentimental glissando. Kate Buchanan rose and sat with the rest. She did not weep. The fat man asked an old man in the congregation to dismiss the service, and the old man muttered an unintelligible prayer. The Potters let Gary and Suzanne off at the house and followed the congregation to the cemetery. After, they'd go to Kate Buchanan's house with casseroles and molds of Jell-O and the church's thirty-cup coffeemaker.

"Alone at last!" Suzanne said.

Gary did not smile, did not kiss her, did not touch her.

"All right, Gary," she said. "Or shall I call you Herbert Gary while you're here in your home territory? I have a right to know what's going on, too." *Ain't I your wife, Herbert Gary?* she almost said, shocked at the mocking she heard in her mind.

"You're right," he said.

Gary had moved north, beyond this smoky little Egypt, she thought, but he still belonged here.

"We're going to have to stay here a little while," he said. "I just couldn't tell you. What with the new baby. But they let me go. The

Little Egypt

new management shook things up, promoted Albie, shit-canned a bunch of us."

"Oh honey," she said. "Why couldn't you tell me that?"

"I thought I could borrow from Dad. We could hang on for a little while in the apartment then, while I found something else. But Dad, he just doesn't have it. He said he'd take out a loan, but I can't have him do that. We don't have anything left from your trip."

She looked down at the baby kicking quietly on the brown couch.

"Now don't look like that," Gary said. "I'm not blaming you. I'm happy we have her. Really I am. It'll just be for a little while here. I'll go back to Chicago, sweet-talk the landlord, find something. Then we'll be back where we were."

Wherever that was, she thought.

Olin left for several days' work in Cairo, pronounced Cayro, and Gary returned to Chicago, leaving her in foreign territory. The baby slept in a portable crib that Francine Grace borrowed from Kate Buchanan. "I kind of hated to ask," Francine Grace said. "But it's not like she done anything. She was friendly as could be. Said, 'You may as well have the crib. I ain't having no more babies.' Like to broke my heart. When I went in that kitchen, I see where there's blood on the wallpaper."

Suzanne began learning lessons from her mother-in-law.

"See here," Francine Grace said, setting the supper table, "when there's a hole in the tablecloth, you put the saltshaker over it."

With a scarf tied under her chin, she danced shuffling across the rug. "See, what you do is walk like this across the yard and shuffle up the leaves and then they blow to the neighbors' yard."

She held the baby and held the baby. "Some people says you oughtn't to baby them too much," she said. "Olin, he'd whop Herbert Gary on occasion. But I just think a mother has got to gentle them."

She whisked through the living room with a hot pink feather duster. To the tune of "O Tannenbaum," she sang, "Oh Feather Duster, oh how I love thee."

She bought a good length of pink rosebud flannel, drew a pattern on newspaper, and stitched together a half-dozen kimonos on an old black Singer.

"And you always feed the last bite of anything to the dog," she said.

She met the homely black dog's long stare. "Who's in there?" she asked. "Who's in there?" She said she believed the little dog's body held someone reincarnated.

"I know your mother-in-law cannot replace your mother," she said. "But I hope we can be close."

The night before Gary returned, Suzanne patted the baby to sleep in the borrowed crib and sat holding an open book and watching situation comedies with Francine Grace. "You know, I appreciate your taking care of us," Suzanne said. "I mean, my mother would have been organizing job hunts and clipping coupons and telling me what to do. She always had these expectations. It was so hard to please her."

Francine Grace said nothing, only laughed at the television and asked her if she'd ever used the laundry powder in the commercial. Suzanne went to Gary's childhood bedroom at 10:30 with her betrayal in her ears. She put on her robe and lingered in the hall, organizing the words to tell Francine Grace that she loved her mother but unable to say anything but good-night, see you in the morning.

She stroked the baby's back. She thought of Kate Buchanan stroking her babies in the same crib and wondered if she'd foreseen the single-barreled shotgun and the spattered wallpaper in her kitchen. Your mother-in-law cannot replace your dead mother, she told herself. She wondered if Gary lay awake remembering morning oatmeal and after-school cowboys with Bucky, pondering the various ways people abandoned their homes.

The next day, Gary came for her and the baby. It hadn't been so hard after all, he said. All that worry, and he'd got right on at McFarland's and they'd given him an advance and he'd paid up the rent. He brought two bottles of champagne, a case of beer, and a plush bear. "I shouldn't have worried," he said. "I guess this old country boy can handle old Chi-town all right."

Olin returned from Cairo. He'd spent an extra day out, hunting. "But I ain't bringing no dinner," he said. "Clarence, he's the only one even got off a shot. I kicked up a covey and they gone right over his head. He brought one down and then had to shoot it in the head with his pistol. Let me tell you what he done: he gutted it and eat the heart. Said the mountain men and the Indians done it and he always wanted to."

Suzanne wanted to talk to Kate Buchanan before they left. Little Egypt meant something, and she needed to know the message. She had the lessons from Francine Grace. Still, she thought Dexter Donald's wife could make some connection for her.

In the evening, she stood in the brown leaf-covered yard alone. The sky was spread in horizontal bands behind a bare water oak: dark orange heavy on the earth, rising into yellow-white and then luminous blue, seeping into deep blue. Wisps of clouds rose in the luminous blue band, and she thought of her mother's kissed tissues rising in the hot air of the bathroom register. *Cleft for me,* she thought, not knowing in what she wanted to hide herself: the Potters, or the banded sky, or the ancient country around her, or Mt. Hope Mausoleum.

Kate Buchanan walked toward her down the gravel road in front of the Potters' house. She said nothing until she reached Suzanne. "You're Francine Grace's daughter-in-law, right?" she asked solemnly. "You and Herbert Gary got that new baby, right?"

Suzanne nodded. *Daughter-in-law* was altogether different from *daughter,* she thought. *I'll never be anyone's daughter ever again,* she thought.

"I just wanted to know, do you need any things for that baby?" Kate said. "Emmadine said it's a orphan you sprung from the Philippine Islands. I figured you could use maybe the stroller. I got stuff I ain't ever going to be needing—a bottle warmer and a little tub, this, that, and the other thing."

Kate Buchanan stood in the darkening yard and began crying. "My boys is three and four," she said. "I ain't cried until now. You don't know me. It's like Dexter Donald eat my heart out."

Suzanne stood with her while she wept, not presuming to touch her or say anything. Finally she said, "My mother just died. I know it isn't the same. But I can tell you this: he didn't really eat your heart out." She pictured her father-in-law's friend Clarence chewing the tiny quail heart and swallowing. "You wouldn't be crying like this if you didn't have some heart left. And you have enough heart for your kids, I can tell that."

"Everybody figures I was a lousy wife. That's why he done it."

"Oh no," Suzanne said. "That isn't true. Listen: I've heard them talking. Nobody blames you. They're only concerned for you. I promise."

Look, she wanted to say to Kate, and pull the fading layers of sky around them. *You're a real daughter here, and they love you. And me: they've taken me in and Sara Grace too,* and she felt Gary's land banding her.

"No one dies because of someone else," she said. "People just die when they have to, one way or the other. It wasn't our fault." Maybe Dexter Donald couldn't take the pull of the dank land, the ancient blooded land, and couldn't escape its gravity. It held Gary, too, but as something to spin away from, to home in on. She'd had no lodestone but her mother. She thought of Dexter Donald dead in the earth, carbonizing in the wet earth. She thought of her mother in the mausoleum, dry and light as bones.

In the morning, she and Gary loaded the car, hugged Olin and Francine Grace, and took their daughter north, potent with the motion of coming from, going to. Suzanne held her daughter to the gravity of her heart.

The Kiss

MARTIN had actually kissed Molly only once, the first time. The curves of their lives grazed each other maybe once a year, when they managed to meet at a conference somewhere away from their homes. Their spouses knew enough to smell something fishy. Molly suspected she looked guilty when she returned to Chet, and she could hardly stop the tiny smile, smug and contrite, from reddening her, even as she truthfully denied all. And she was sorry for that tick of hurt.

This time they met in Florida, where everything was steamy and green and salty, and Molly's hair kinked up. He spread his arms when he spotted her in the lobby, and she walked into him and took the hug. Convalescence flooded her, when she'd believed she was finished with all that, and she blotted her eyes on his shoulder.

"Molly-Polly," he said, "oh my Molly-Polly. I really need to talk to you." His hair was longer than it had been last year in San Diego, and Molly wondered if the friz was his new style or the humidity. He had thickened a little, and his clothes were too heavy for Florida in August.

"Martin? What's wrong?"

She liked saying his name, making the soft T against the back of her teeth. She didn't call her husband by name. She didn't know when she'd stopped, but now the silence was too thick to take in the spoken word Chet. When she said his name in his absence, his T was hard enough against her teeth to make another syllable. She called him Sweetheart. Martin's wife called him Marty.

"Let's check in. Get registered. I'll tell you all about it later."

"I've been waiting to talk with you, too," she said. She hadn't been able to quit her peppy good-faced Molly act with anyone, it had been too private, too singular for anyone but Chet, and he had no patience for graceless pain.

After the morning sessions, they met for lunch and found a pair of seats at a round table with no one they knew. "I'd just as soon stay away from my colleagues for the duration," Martin said. "Tongues are already a-waggle."

"Chet calls them my miniature colleagues," she said.

Everybody in the ballroom wore printed nametags, and many had crossed out the legal name and like politicians added the good-old names. At their table, Harold was Hal, Lowell was Bud, Edith was Edie, and Gladys was Shivani. They exchanged where-you-froms (Connecticut, Indiana, Alabama . . .) and just-got-back-froms (London, Fiji, my ashram . . .). They ate their salads, pushed aside the ham from the cordon bleu, and raptly spooned up mousse as the famous speaker spoke.

"Look at that," Molly whispered to Martin, making a quick gesture at the plates with the pink scorned ham. "Looks like they spit out their tongues." She shut up when Shivani gave her an Eastern glare.

But I don't care how superior you are, she thought, hot and guilty, I'm plain old Molly, and I am still alive.

The kiss. Martin had danced with her at the first-night mixer in Chicago. Years ago. Her body was sound then, sound of wind and limb, as Chet would say. Martin led her down to the lakeshore, and fuzzy from the free drinks in the hospitality rooms, she floated along, tethered to his hand. They moved from their jobs to their families to his two-year sobriety to his life adrift. "I know what you mean," she said. And she did. She was committed to her work, she and Chet loved each other solidly, but sometimes she was thinly shrouded, against what she did not know. "We're in this together," she told Martin. "You and I." They stood against each other in the sand in the dark. The lake had receded that year, and she could smell dead fish. She wondered why the fish didn't simply stay with the water as it shrank into its own depths. But maybe they'd been trapped by sandbars. She didn't know. Martin kissed her. They were in this together. After a moment, though, she turned her head. "Okay," he said. With her eyes closed, she was dizzy. That was all.

The Kiss

She needed to open her eyes and breathe, that was all, and then they would resume. But he said, "Okay," believing he understood her fidelity to her own life. Every year they held hands and confided the previous months' enlightenments and losses. She didn't know if he even desired to kiss her again.

Molly went to her seminar in the afternoon and Martin to his. After, she changed into her white sundress, leaving the room neat in case he returned with her later, and waited with a glass of house wine in the bar. Martin still didn't drink. She watched him search for her in the darkened bar, find her, walk in the midst of all the cocktail strangers, her good friend Martin in his tropical shirt. It wouldn't be anything to Chet, anything at all, if having survived her disease she kissed Martin. She could feel his cotton shirt and his khakis under her palms.

They pushed through the dense night until they found a seafood restaurant. Inside, they shivered in their damp clothes. The waiter set down oysters and rubbed his hands in anticipation of their pleasure.

"Okay, you first, Molly-Polly." Martin rubbed his palms together, teasing about the waiter, yes, but eager to tell his buttered story too.

Suddenly she was shy about the cancer. It wasn't his pity she wanted, even his sympathy. Chet had been sympathetic enough, and after half a year, the terrible details of IV, mesh panties, vomiting, liquid diet, men screaming down the hall, catheter, greasy hair, pain, of course pain, at night the septic light from the hall and the hands every two hours turning and testing and medicating all night and whispering on her old rubber skin—the terrible details had blurred as she came back to life.

"It's really nothing," she said to Martin. "It's not worth dwelling on. I only wanted to tell you, that's all. I had cancer, is the thing. I had surgery, though, and I'm all right now."

Immediately he reached for her hand across the table. "That's scary. That's really scary. Why didn't you write or call and tell me? When was this? I'd have sent you some flowers or something, anyway."

"I had plenty of flowers. I didn't want for sympathy."

The waiter came for their orders and Molly smiled at him in relief. Chet had mostly stayed away from the hospital, and all the flowers had come from her miniature colleagues and friends. She hadn't wanted Chet to see her vomiting in a basin or looking so greasy and so—well, so mortal. But he hadn't been in it with her. He'd seen her laughing her way into surgery and by the time he picked her up, her hair was washed and she was joking with the nurses.

"Tell me about you," she said to Martin. She still wanted to show him her vitality. That was the lesson of it all, anyway. Be vital in the flesh together.

"I'm in love," he said.

Their waiter set up his tray and handed over their sizzling plates. "Enjoy, folks. Save room for dessert. Think key lime."

"This is a tourist place," Martin said after he left.

"So what? We're tourists."

"Everybody thinks I'm terrible," he said. "Just having the usual mid-life crisis. My wife is the only one who doesn't know yet. She's a good person, you know? A man couldn't want a better wife, really. So I don't know what to do. Wait till Christopher gets through high school, I guess. That would be right. But Naomi—she's this dancer, she's fantastic—but she's—younger. She has this little boy I'm nuts about. I'm all torn up."

Molly forked shrimp around on her plate. It was impossible that the white rubber flesh had been alive. "I'm not one to advise you," she said. Chet might swallow up some Naomi, too, and Molly herself had been going after full body contact, hadn't she. Martin was only trying to stay in the shallows.

"I'm not looking for an answer," he said. "I just needed to tell you. I knew you'd understand. After all, we're in this together. Let's have us some dessert, hey?"

Outside, the steamy dark engulfed her. She raised the back of her hand to her lips. Of course she was in it alone. Of course. She opened her mouth and touched her tongue to her skin. It was salty. It was sweet.

Comparative Demographics of
A.M. & P.M. Transit Riders

THE true bus people didn't come out until dusk. The morning people were like children pretending to be grown-ups. This was the way of big people—nodding at each other at the butt-littered bus stop, saying, "This darn rain," smoothing the corners of their dollar bills so they would be gulped readily into the bus's money-sucking machine. Schlooop down the hatch. The big people boarded the bus in single file and took the same seats every morning. Then they unfolded a newspaper or opened a briefcase until they looked up and noticed their stop. These were the ways of grown-ups.

Connie kept waiting for the business of their morning sobriety to be jiggled by the bus's vibrations and lurches into the jerky movements of children, a nose wiped down a sweater sleeve, a wet giggle behind a hand.

Connie might have been one of them, to look at her sober face, her walking shoes.

Once she rode all the way to the unknown city of San Jose. The lost city of San Jose. She told the people at work she was so absorbed in a book that she missed her stop by miles. In truth she was dopey with sobriety, nearly dozing. At least her legs had stopped itching for a while. And being late for work and losing two hours' pay was almost worth that.

She wondered if the big people in the morning were transformed by the dusk, whether the same creatures, preparing their faces for the business of the morning, shook themselves in the evening and stretched until they became the dusk people.

But no. What did they do with their white blouses and their sport jackets? How would their leather briefcases get home?

In the early evening, she waited in the rain, beneath the bland gray sky. *Don't talk to anyone on the bus,* her husband told her every morning. *Be careful,* he said.

When the bus farted to a stop, she climbed on, dripping down the aisle, and squeezed herself among the night bus people. There were no habits on the evening bus. She reached under one pant leg and then the other and scratched, thinking that if she let her fingernails grow there might be more relief. When she lifted her hands to open the book, she saw blood under her nails.

At the back of the bus two boys were questioning a creature with a face bearded as a Schnauzer's.

"Where you goin', man?" one boy said, a smirk in his voice.

"Somewhere, man," he answered in an exaggerated Mexican accent. "Anywhere."

"You don't know?"

"I never know," he said.

"Well, what you do, man?"

Connie turned to look at them. The boys were about twelve years old, she guessed. The hairy man wore three coats that she could see, with a tightly strung hood covering his head, forehead, and chin.

"I travel," he said, this time without the accent. "I'm the traveler."

The boys giggled. The man at the back of the bus began enumerating the cities he'd traveled to. *Chicago, Baltimore, Gainesville, St. Louis, all on the bus, man, Kankakee, New Orleans.*

Connie opened her book and heard the rhythm of the traveler's cities.

"Hey man, my grandma lives in Orlando," one of the boys said. "You know my Grandma Cooper?"

"I've been to Orlando," the man said. "Sure I know your grandmother."

"Oh wow," the boys said to each other. "Jesus."

Indianapolis, Kalamazoo, Seattle, Silver Springs.

Connie used to ride a bus to school when she was in second grade. She and Jeanette Gamber would meet in the field across from the bus stop. Every week they'd bring a balled-up pair of socks or white cotton panties or even a sweater, and they'd disinter their cache. In the spring they began hiding cans of green beans or tomato soup in their book satchels and then burying the cans in the field, too. When it was time to run away, they would be ready. They could travel and wander away from their mothers and fathers for a long time. Or they could hide out in the woods. Build a treehouse. They waited for the morning when they were both sufficiently mad at their parents. Once Jeanette arrived crying and threw down a can of pork and beans, ready to take their supplies and go. But after school she allowed Connie to convince her that her mom didn't mean it, and went on home to the green-shingled Gamber house. The next year they went to third grade at a new school. The cardboard box of little girls' clothes and canned food remained in its shallow hole in that overgrown field. In third grade she and Jeanette were no longer best friends, but neither told about the box, ever, or took it and ran away.

"Why you get off here, man?" one of the boys said.

"Hey, Traveler," the other boy yelled out the window, "you been to Alaska?"

The man with the hairy face turned in the rain and bowed toward the bus.

The bus emptied as it continued north. She was left sitting by a black man in a navy blue watch cap. If she moved across the aisle to sit and scratch her legs alone, he'd think her prejudiced. Or his feelings would be hurt at the apologetic smile she could feel her lips readying.

The back of the seat in front of them read "Soul bites the big one" and "Kome rules." Across from them a small plastic trident occupied a seat beside an old man hawking into a yellow Kleenex. Wrappers and day passes skittered down the aisle when the bus stopped.

"The first time she got away with it," a girl's voice said from the back of the bus. "The second time she got suspended."

What? What was it possible to get away with, at least once?

"What're you reading?" the man beside her asked, and her mouth, unprepared for the contortions of speaking, closed. She held the book up for him to see for himself.

"What's the best book you've ever read?" he said.

Connie could hear her husband: *Don't talk to men on the bus. Be careful.* But books . . .

"That takes some thought," she said. She liked the neat dark blue knit cap on his head.

"No, it doesn't," he said. "Doesn't take a second. Hemingway. *For Whom the Bell Tolls.* No question."

They debated the man of action for several blocks. At least he went to Africa and Spain, she thought. He wouldn't have stood the agonies of madly itching legs.

"What I don't like, though," the man beside her said, "is how he glorified war. I've been in a war, and it is *not* the way he writes it."

She reached down to scratch her left calf, and when she leaned back in her seat again, she saw that there were tears running down his cheeks. "People hear I've been to Viet Nam, and they want to know have I killed anybody. Oh I killed some, oh yes," he said, mumbling in a wet voice, and he went on nearly inaudibly, crying and mumbling. "Do . . . look like a killer to you? . . . Yeah, I killed . . ."

"Listen, I've got to get off," she said. She reached across him and pressed the yellow buzzer strip.

". . . I look like? . . ."

"No," she told him. "No, you don't."

She left him and walked to the back of the bus. When the green light above the door flashed, she pushed open the doors and stepped down onto the street.

She walked the three blocks to the flat-topped rented house where her husband would be sitting in the chair by the door watching the news. There would be a martini beside him on top of the stereo speaker.

She walked fast, not running in panic, but as if laughing people awaited her. *Walk like you have a destination,* her husband said. *It's safer than uncertainty or aimlessness.*

Inside the house, she said, "How was your day?" And winced. Why did she allow words like those to emerge? Why were they inside her in the first place?

"Same old shit," he said.

From the kitchen ten minutes later, she heard him burst out: "Damn!"

She watched her feet move her back to the front room. "What's the matter?" she said. Who was the programmer who had locked in all these woman-phrases?

"Goddamn congressmen voted themselves another raise," he said. "They didn't notice it. Just tacked onto a black lung bill. Didn't notice it. Ha."

In the morning, he said, "Come over here. I want you to look at this egg. Hard. Rubber. Do you think just once you could shock me and get it right?"

Three fried eggs. Every morning. The yolks broke when she turned the eggs. Or solidified before she even tried turning them. As if she did it on purpose. Maybe she did.

She rolled up one of her old T-shirts and stuffed it into her book bag.

"Be careful," her husband said.

She walked to the bus stop oh so carefully. She sat among the morning people, quiescent in the clean bus. She got off at the same stop that she did every single morning. At the fence between the railroad tracks and the road, she pushed aside the thick, littered bushes and dug a shallow hole with one foot. She buried the T-shirt and then headed across the block-long parking lot of the plant, and inside she sat on her green vinyl swivel chair, pushing the proper buttons and itching.

In the evening she boarded the dirty bus.

"May I talk to you about Jesus?" a young black man said to a jaundiced-looking white man.

"Why not?" he answered.

Connie liked the proselytizer's hat. It was a tan derby with an index card with "Jesus Saves" hand-lettered on it stuck on the hat like a press card.

You'd never catch morning people wearing hats. The dusk people wore knitted fisherman's caps and light green bowlers with red feathers at the side. Or they wore headphones like hats, with the radios off for conversations. Or they wore their hair like hats— bushy, in elaborate cornrows and ropes, in spikes.

An old woman leaned over to Connie. "You see a doctor about them legs," she whispered, and then labored to the front of the bus, leaning like a climber against the slowing motion.

Connie was sitting between two women. The one on her left said, "Did you know I went to school with one of Manson's girls? Susan Atkins. Junior high."

The one on her right said, "Don't tell nobody. But I think I'm p.g. My old man's gonna kill me."

Funny how bus riders traveling with people they knew rarely conversed. But single riders confided anything, sometimes just routes and late buses or the goddamned rain, but as often dead brothers or unfaithful husbands or children lost.

"I'm thinking of leaving my husband," she told the women flanking her.

"You ought to shave your legs, honey, if you're going to wear shorts," the one on the right said across Connie to the other. "No offense."

The other hitched her bra strap back onto her shoulder and took no offense.

"It's not that there's anything wrong with him," Connie said. "Oh, he's so cynical and pessimistic. But so what?"

"I left my husband once," the woman with the hairy legs said. "For thirteen days."

The other woman nudged Connie. "Look at that Chinese baby," she said. "Oh I just love those little ornamental kids."

When Connie got off the bus she looked over her shoulder to see if anyone had gotten off after her. *Always check to see if anybody's following you,* her husband would say. The shadows kept their places among the bushes until she was inside.

"How was your day?" she said.

"Same old shit," he said.

The morning people knew each other well—where each would sit, who would command the driver to have a nice day upon disembarking. They knew each other's workday wardrobes. The only uncertainty was in which of her four styles the blonde girl would wear her hair.

Where Connie got off, there was a sandwich in a bread wrapper on the ground by the road. It had lain on that gravel for nine days.

She walked across the same huge parking lot of the plant every morning at 8:08. There was the same blue sign: DRIVERS CHOCK

Comparative Demographics of a.m. & p.m. Transit Riders

YOUR WHEELS. Inside, her supervisor walked fast and stiffly to the men's room. "Teeth are floating," he said as he did every morning. "All that coffee."

She settled into her green vinyl swivel chair before her same tan and gray machine, initialized it, and began working the same orange keys.

This was why people had affairs. This was why people had children. Why people argued and made up. Left their husbands. Took little trips into the city or down the coast. Boarded the morning bus one day carrying a tie in their hands instead of wearing it. Temporary relief from the same old, same old. Why they first said, "I'll have a dry martini." Tried wearing their hair up one morning.

But then these alterations grew into the same old, as the martinis appeared nightly on the stereo speaker beside you and you got the four hairstyles down to a weekly pattern, you rushed to the bus stop holding your tie every morning, you decided to have another baby when Timmy was out of diapers and into play school—why all those affairs tasted alike on the desensitized palate.

On the morning bus, with a nearly toeless pair of knee socks balled at the bottom of her book bag, Connie looked through her billfold pictures. Mom and Dad unsmiling under opaque plastic. A young man sitting sideways on a motorcycle, on his face the awareness that he could swing one leg over and ride off at any time. Daniel before she'd known him. Dan in the midwest, a spring green cornfield behind him, before the same old three-olive martini (meal in a glass, he said), the same old wife, the same old life. He didn't care, he said. But the boy in the white Levis, leaning onto a motorcycle, cared.

Pictures. Some nieces' baby pictures with make-up smears on the plastic over them.

A honeymoon couple, stiff and grinning, beside flamingos. And we know who this pair is, don't we, fellow riders? Yes, that's Connie and Dan on their honeymoon, when nothing was the same, when no one was old but other people.

There should be other photographs, too. She remembered walking all afternoon with that new husband, both of them timid about bargaining for their souvenirs, although you were supposed to, and how her new sandals had worn the skin from her feet until she was leaving a trail of blood behind. She hadn't wanted to say anything.

She remembered the two of them in lounge chairs in the hot flamingo night, drinking coco-locos. She had a picture in her head now of that bride stretched out on a webbed chair, with her bloody feet, holding onto a coconut with a straw in it, and crying. She'd never been able to tell him why the bride had cried and cried.

Look at them in the daytime picture. They were ordinary people even then. You can see that their honeymoon clothes were new. You can see small creases in their flesh, the faint acne scars, the moles, the one eye smaller than the other, the whiskers: you can see they wore their bodies uncertainly then.

In the meantime, she'd stopped crying. She'd begun frying three eggs a morning. She'd taken her small promotions and moved onto the green vinyl swivel chair at work. Life in a glass—fill it, sip it for years over ice, walk anesthetized to and fro.

The rain had washed away most of the dirt over the buried T-shirt. The old shirt, sodden and muddy, lay behind the bushes like the pieces of discarded clothing you see anywhere: an orlon sweater hung on a bush, a gray pair of men's underwear buddied up to a curb. Were they waiting for runaways? She threw the socks behind the bushes. If she'd meant it, she would have buried her blue wool sweater, her favorite jeans, not clothes waiting to be next week's rags.

The evening bus people looked aimless. The teenagers hopped off and on, flashing day passes, as whim decreed. The old men and women in their hats, the crippled and bent people with their crooked arms and walkers in the aisle, the fat people with the flesh bunched above their ankle socks like double chins—they all rode somewhere as the Traveler did. *Moving* was the preventative for itching legs.

On the final day she didn't bother hiding old clothes in her book bag. On the bus south to work she opened a book, and wondered about the ordinary lives of the neat weekday people riding with her and about their remedies, and scratched her legs.

Comparative Demographics of a.m. & p.m. Transit Riders

At her usual stop, the bus swung over and stopped.
She had not pressed the yellow strip of the buzzer.
She sat still in the blue plastic seat.
"Here's your stop," the driver called back to her. "I guess you were too into your book to notice."
Yes, I was really into that book, she said, yes thanks for stopping. So much for a passive remedy. She disembarked and stepped past the dead sandwich and walked her itching legs across the parking lot.
Drivers chock your wheels.
And at the other end of the day she embarked upon the short trip home, seating herself at the back of the bus where the seats were arranged like a conversation pit.
"That must be a hell of an itch," an Indian man across from her said.
A fat man in overalls said, "I bet I could cure it."
She stared at the fat man with a nobody-touches-me look, thinking he'd have to cut away an inch of carrion from her before he got to live meat anyway.
"Listen," she said, "I want to ask you all something: don't you ever get tired of the same old thing every day?"
The fat man began nodding vigorously, working up to speech, as if she'd accepted his proposition. "Age," he said. "Age is just a number. Me," he said, still nodding, "me, I feel sixteen. Physically. Sexually. Mentally."
"When I get tired, I just ride on up to Berserkely," the man from India said. He giggled.
"I hear you, sweetheart," a woman said. "My name's Hattie. You know what? Every morning I stand in front of Ernie's Antiques and wait for the same old bus. And every morning there comes along a woman, must be in her sixties, comes walking along holding this man's hand and sweet-talking him along. He's walking and watching his feet, kind of humped-over. He's maybe forty and all chubby like a kid. I watch them every morning and she shows him every morning how to watch for the walk light and she buttons up his sweater and puts him onto a bus across the street. Every morning."
Hattie put her chin in her palm and looked sideways, knowing

and smug, at Connie. "Same old thing, right? I figure he's her retarded kid. So one morning I say to the kid, 'That sweater sure is a pretty blue.' And he just fingers the buttons on his pretty blue sweater. But the mom just grins away at me and now every morning we'll say something, she'll say, 'That a good magazine?' or I'll say, 'Doesn't this rain get to you?' But here's the real thing: I listen to her and she just talks to that big empty kid and teaches him the same things every day and points out the dandelions in the sidewalk to him and the orange centers of the palms or whatever."

Hattie nodded, *so there,* satisfied with the lesson, and turned to press the yellow buzzer strip.

"My name's Tommy," the fat man in overalls confided. "What's yours?"

"Constance," she said.

"I like you," Tommy said. "Nobody ever likes me, you know."

She smiled and stood to get off the bus. Now there'd be a real mission in life, she thought, something to commit oneself to—give all these hopeless, fat and deformed and old men a little gratification. She pushed the bus doors open when the green light above them lit up. Give self-confidence to some of the lost ones, Nightingale among the derelicts. Yes, a worthy cause, a noble cause. Put a smile on those hopeless faces, a memory in those helpless bodies.

Don't suppose Daniel would approve, she thought. Maybe he'd throw her out when he found out. You're sick, sick, sick, he'd say to her, couldn't be satisfied with my good, ordinary loving, could you? Had to go out and find something different. Sick, sick. She could almost feel his hands on her shoulders, shaking her until her neck loosened obediently.

"I really like you," someone said right behind her.

She jumped guiltily, guilty of sick thoughts, guilty of failure to be careful.

"Leave me alone," she said. "Go on, get out of here." She stepped up her pace, not running from the fat man but walking as if she had a mission. She turned the corner onto the sidewalk of her own street.

Then Tommy was beside her, on the curb side like a gentleman, and he fell on her, pushing her sideways into the bushes. Just as they smashed through the bushes, the street lights blinked on. Connie could not breathe with the fat man on her. Sticks punctured her back. Daniel, come out now, Daniel, she thought, unable to draw screaming breath. Tommy reached under her neck with his fat right hand and unhooked the overall strap from his rounded left shoulder. Keeping her flattened on the dirt, he reversed the move and unfastened the other strap.

Tommy at mental age sixteen, mental and physical and sexual age sixteen, she thought, Tommy sick and fat pressing his fat on her chest as he reached down to work on the button at the hip of the overalls. *Nobody ever likes me.* He wriggled on her like an enormous slug in the dusk of her own street, nobody in the houses seeing them beneath the street lights, Daniel sitting with a martini in front of the television, unable to receive her messages.

She was attempting to shift him up, imagining her teeth in the fat white meat of the shoulder, when he said, "Oh shit. Oh goddamn it. Shit." He heaved off her and stood beside her with his unbuttoned overalls halfway down and caught on his belly.

Connie began breathing again, taking shallow breaths carefully until her chest loosened after the pressure of the fat man's weight.

When she opened her eyes Tommy was crying with vigorous childish heaves. He opened his arms in the dusk and she could see the wet front of his undropped overalls.

Daniel, she croaked, and sat up beside the smashed bushes.

Tommy lumped off down the block. She watched him lurch around the corner with his overall bib flapping.

Connie sat with her legs straight out. The smashed bushes began to plump up and rise around her. Across the street and down the block she saw the porch light of her house come on, not suddenly as the brittle street lights had, at the moment of the fall, but softly. She watched the darkness around the porch light yielding. The front door opened and Daniel stepped out.

He could not rescue her.

But that had never been the sort of love she'd imagined anyway. He was no more a man than he had been among the flamingos of their honeymoon when she had sat before him crying uselessly. He had settled quickly into their life.

She loved him. He could not save her. And she loved him.

The secret of the night people was that they'd stopped expecting. No more new hairdos, no more overhanging blouses to hide the fat, no more jogging during the lunch hour, no more briefcases and best-selling novels. They'd let go. They rolled along with the bus.

She held her hand above the rising leaves of the bush beside her until they touched her palm.

That was the deliverance. Her life was her own. Unchock your wheels. Be there for the rising leaves, unwaiting but open-palmed.

Serpentine

THE first snake intruded the night Denny went along with his office crew to the girlie bars. She hadn't minded that he'd gone, not really, picturing girl after overripe girl squirming on her portable rug like a kindergartner on a pallet at rest period. What would the girl think of Denny's deadened eyes on her, if she thought at all? Abruptly, Sheila saw her own deadened eyes watching him, and she thought the girl's eyes would be condescending on them both: it ain't much, she might think with a grind, but at least it's life.

The snake stretched down the toilet tank, all the way down into the bowl, with his head just out of the water. A bit of toilet paper stuck to the side of his head like papier-mâché. He was thin and dark gray, about three feet long. He hadn't moved when she switched on the light in the master bathroom, and she'd been mildly curious, not afraid. She knew he was a non-poisonous rat snake, the only kind on the island. She switched off the light, closed the door, and blocked the crack under the door with rags.

In the morning, Denny told her about the girls at the bars and how they'd all dragged off the runway the instant the music stopped, blank and slack as someone in a house alone, heading for the toilet. She told him about the snake, and when they cautiously opened the bathroom door, broom ready, the snake had gone.

"He had to have gone down the toilet," Denny said. "There's no other way out."

She shuddered. "Oh, what if I'd just plunked myself down without turning on the light."

It made a good story at work. Denny had told it all around. "I told them that it sort of discourages sitting there with the morning paper," he said.

When the second snake intruded four days later, they were sitting up in bed, reading, a habit from the old days which still felt friendly enough. Sheila slid out of bed and headed for the bathroom, saying, "Look out all you snakes, here comes the big bad mama." She heard the words, and hoped Denny wouldn't fix on them, remembering that she was nobody's mama any more. They didn't talk about that. In the toilet, a snake was just emerging. His head was out of the water, and the body was sliding out of the hole.

She didn't scream, the way women were supposed to do. "Oh my God," she said, low, "there *is* one."

"Get the broom," Denny said, and she ran for it.

Before the snake had emerged more than halfway, Denny reached over and hit the flush lever. Instead of being sucked back, the snake came flying up. Denny thrust the broom at him, and he slid over the low wall to the shower stall. Denny thrust and the snake struck the broom straws, corkscrewing his body, opening his hinged jaws, hissing like a panther, and striking.

"Oh, let's just block off the bathroom again," Sheila said.

Denny thrust and thrust. "Get the machete," he said.

"Oh, why kill him?" she said. "I don't like snakes, but still he's harmless. It's only a rat snake. Just let him leave when he's ready. We'll quit using this bathroom. We can walk around to the other one."

Denny struck with the broom and the snake started toward him. "Maybe you're right," he said, and pulled the door closed.

In the morning, they opened the bathroom door, and of course he was gone. But the soap dish was in the sink and the perfume bottles she kept lined up on the top of the toilet tank were fallen and scattered.

"I didn't do that last night," Denny said. "I know that."

In fact, she thought, they hadn't done much of anything last night.

Sheila emptied the medicine chest and cleared off the perfume bottles. Denny sprayed insecticide in the shower drain and into the toilet bowl. They closed the door once more and stuffed the old diapers she kept for rags under the door. They began keeping a flashlight by the bed so that they could find their way to the other bathroom in the night without lighting up the whole house.

The third snake was a joke. They were trying to read to the fluctuating light, the surge and draw of the power lighting and dimming the pages, when Denny said, "There's a snake coming out from under the bathroom door."

"Oh no," she said. "Is there really?"

"No," he said. "Just joking."

She checked the diapers under the door anyway. She laughed. He didn't make many jokes any more. It wasn't funny, but she laughed. "Don't *do* that to me," she said.

"What *can* I do to you then?" he said.

"Anything you like," she said. "You know that. I just didn't know you liked it any more." She wedged a diaper farther under the bathroom door. Her bare skin felt puffy, her body inflated with emptiness.

"It's hard to get in the mood sometimes," he said.

"Oh, I know," she said. She thought that a woman would cry now. "I do know."

They'd moved to the island three months ago, after Denny's company had agreed to the transfer. They could not live in San Francisco any longer, especially with each other. Their friends avoided them, unable to take the tension of the grief or the inability to find healing words or the gratitude that their own children were alive. And the slant of the northern light reminded her always of the afternoon Scottie died. The island's light shimmered in the heat, and sometimes Sheila felt dizzy with the motion, as if the island were floating, but most of the time she and Denny both were distracted enough by the changed life to believe they had forgotten the death and their separate guilts. The tropical heat and brightness kept them lethargic and too sweaty to touch each other.

The next snake intruded in the morning, when Denny was at work. Sheila was making the bed when she caught a glimpse of motion. The old diaper she'd stuffed under the bathroom door was moving. She shuddered and pushed the diaper back with her bare foot.

Abruptly the radio in the living room died, and the bedroom fan slowed and then stopped.

The diaper moved and two snakes' heads appeared, pushing against the rag. Sheila pulled the bedroom door closed behind her, but there was a two-inch crack under that door, also. She grabbed more rags and stuffed them beneath the door. From the storage room she dragged two heavy wooden packing crates and pushed them against the bedroom door.

Denny called at noon. "Have you listened to any news? There's a typhoon warning." She said nothing, thinking only of the two snakes' heads pushing the cloth, abreast like a two-headed creature. "It's all right," Denny said. "The storm's a ways out still and it may not even hit us. But I'll stop on the way home and get in some supplies."

"The power's off again," she said.

"Oh great," Denny said. "Well, I'll get more batteries and some candles. We'll live."

"Yes, I suppose we will," she said.

"Hey now," he said. "We're doing all right. Aren't we now?"

She didn't tell him about the snakes. She guessed she could cope with a couple of harmless rat snakes. In the early afternoon she mopped the tile floors. The water trickled and then spat from the faucet when she filled the bucket the final time, and she wondered if the power failure could affect the water pressure. She set pitchers in the sink and let the thin stream from the faucet fill them.

The morning had been bright, and she'd thought about hiking down to the beach. The afternoon sky was gray, as if it had waited for Denny's call to confirm the coming storm. Sheila could see whitecaps far out to sea. By three o'clock, sea and sky blended horizonless, and it might have been dusk.

She sat at the kitchen table with a candle burning and tried to write letters home. Their friends had said they mustn't make exiles of themselves, though Sheila had thought she'd seen relief at their leaving. She wrote bright letters, as bright and brittle as the morning had been. They were all right, she wrote. They were healing in the sun. She made jokes about the snakes in the toilet. *Kind of discourages settling down with the morning paper,* she wrote. *See, folks? We're even laughing.*

By four o'clock, she needed two candles at the table. She doodled cartoons of snakes rising from toilet bowls, with balloons above their heads saying *Gotcha!* and *Just when you thought it was safe to go to the bathroom* . . . Foolishness. But the deep dusk outside made the kitchen table and the candlelight and the thick pad of paper and the yellow pencil cozy and familiar and somehow significant. For the first time in five months, she wanted to talk to Brian. She thought about writing to him. I remember your lean body against mine, she would write. I haven't missed you before, she'd tell him. I've been hating you all these months, she'd say. I know your only guilt was your own, when you went home to your wife, but I've been hating you anyway.

She imagined something shredding in the dusk surrounding her, and suddenly she wanted Brian. Then she thought of Denny, returning in the dark to candles. She'd towel the rain from his hair. They'd sit at the kitchen table and drink the California Chardonnay their friends had shipped to them. They'd drive the snakes from the bedroom and maybe hold each other again. She wondered if another child would heal them. In the heavy dusk, she felt warm for men again.

In the bathroom beside the second bedroom, she ran enough warm water to wash. She set the candle on the sink and brushed her hair and powdered her flushed face. Maybe it takes a typhoon to awaken me again, she'd tell Denny. Awaken me from the sleep of the dead.

She prowled out to the carport, looking for Denny's headlights. The tangantangan tree in the yard whipped the dense sky, and the rain shot horizontally past the carport's arches. In the house, she checked the windows, leaving them cracked. She crossed the big window with masking tape. She'd read that the cross of tape would prevent implosion.

She thought about closing the bedroom windows. Perhaps the snakes had exited. The rain would ruin the books and soak the bed. She took the broom, ready to shove back any snakes that appeared when she cracked open the bedroom door. But by the weak flashlight, she saw that one of the packing crates outside the door had already been moved. One end had been pushed about three inches from the door. *Had been pushed,* she thought.

Suddenly drenched with fear, she began searching the house, broom and flashlight in hand. In the guest room, she found a snake under the bed. He stared at her past the flashlight's beam. He did not move, except to throw out his black forked tongue.

Sheila fled the house and waited for Denny in the carport. She could see the luminescent surf spewing up against the rocks. The storm whipped her hair as wildly as the tangantangan branches. She turned off the flashlight to save the weak batteries, every few minutes shining it on the crack under the front door.

In the dark wind, she no longer wanted Brian. She wanted the comfort of Denny—some hazy Denny who years ago, before betrayals, had been able to hold her. And she him. She aimed the flashlight at the crack under the door. She thought of snakes. She thought of Denny doing battle with the snakes. Neither of them had wanted to use the machete. But that had been with one funny snake in the toilet, not this invasion.

Something slogged into the carport then, and she heard herself say *no, no.* She turned the dim light on it and even over the wind heard her husband suck in his breath.

"Jesus!" he said. "Don't ever do that to me. What the devil are you doing out here?"

His hair was wild, and his clothes were soaked and leaf-dotted. He held a shredded umbrella. "Car broke down," he said. "My own damn fault, I guess, going too fast. Water in the distributor cap is all." For now, though, he was dead in the water, he said. The bag of batteries and candles had broken through, and he'd lost everything.

"The house is crawling with snakes," she said.

Crawling with them? How many had she actually seen?

She told him about the packing crates.

"Oh, now, honey," he said.

"You don't believe me," she said.

"How the devil could a skinny old snake move a packing crate? You must have bumped it yourself. It's dark, it's stormy, I was late: you're just over—"

"Wrought," she said. "I'll kill you."

"We've both read Freud," he said. "We've both read D.H. Lawrence. We both know all about snake imagery."

"Is that supposed to be a nasty crack or—" she began, and abruptly stopped and pointed. The snakes were flowing out of the storm over the cinderblock lip of the carport. In reflex, she turned on the flashlight. "Jesus," Denny said. There must have been two dozen black snakes. The light wavered, and she turned it off. Night vision lost, Denny yanked her into the house.

Halfway across the living room, a snake struck her bare ankle. She shrieked and Denny beat the invisible snake until it released her.

"Shh now," he said. "They're not poisonous. At worst you'll get an infection if we don't wash it. Now give me the light."

"No," she whispered. "I need it."

She turned on the dim light and played it around the room. Snakes littered the tile floor like earthworms on a sidewalk after a rain.

"Jesus," Denny said. "Now listen: get up on my back and shine the light ahead of us."

Sheila heard herself whimper. She jumped and wrapped her legs around his hips. Ride the horsie. Denny advanced, waving the ruined umbrella before his feet like a blind man. A snake rose, coiling taut, and Denny caught him on the umbrella and slung him hard against the concrete wall. He fell stunned to the tile.

The two-headed, hump-backed creature advanced, bearing its weak light and its frayed club.

Denny had two snakes hanging from his legs when he reached the guest room. He dumped Sheila on the bed and beat the snakes. He kicked them out the doorway and shut the door.

"Give me that bedspread," he said. "I'm going to block the door. And we'll just sit tight and wait this out. Storm and snakes and all."

"Look under the bed," she said. "Check the closet." She stood on the bed like a dumb broad scared of a mouse. At the window, snakes twisted around the thick banana tree stalk and struck at the screen.

"Nothing under the bed," Denny said. He stripped the sheet from the bed and jammed it under the closet door. Outside, the banana leaves flapped like an awning. Denny sat beside her on the bed.

She giggled. "Get your legs up," she said. "Anything hangs over, the monsters can get it."

"Don't you go hysterical on me," he said. He sat cross-legged facing her. "Now I believe you," he said.

"Scottie would have been terrified," she said.

He looked at her carefully. "Maybe," he said finally. "Or maybe it'd be a big scary game. Or maybe if he were here, they wouldn't be." He reached for her shoulders to pull her to him and she yelled. "What the devil—" he began. She pointed at the bedspread moving slowly away from the door crack. Six snake heads appeared, pushing at the cloth.

"I'd kill for a machete in here," Denny said. Instead he shoved the bedspread back under the door with the point of the umbrella.

Then he turned back to the bed. Sheila sat cross-legged and rigid. Through the storm's incandescence, snakes were crawling up the mattress. "Don't move," Denny said. He reached slowly down into her lap and retrieved the flashlight. "Oh Jesus," he said. Under the bed, snakes dropped from the springs where a nest of dozens writhed. The bedspread and the sheet no longer protected the doors. "Oh Jesus," he said. "Oh Jesus Christ."

A snake struck Sheila then. She leapt from the bed, yanking at the snake with his fangs in her shoulder, dancing and stomping among the snakes on the floor. She jerked open the door and ran, kicking and swinging her arms. And Denny was after her.

They leapt up on the kitchen counter, hurling snakes from their shoulders and legs. Her bare legs bled from the punctures. Their clothes were ripped and bloody from the strikes. But the countertop had a wide overhang, and the snakes trying to climb the cupboards beneath the counter butted their heads and couldn't make the deep right-angle turn upside down. Sheila hopped on the glossy kitchen tile. "Ha hoo! We got them now."

"I'd say it's they who've got us," Denny said.

They stood on their kitchen counter and without the flashlight now watched the black shadows angle and rise and strike at the cupboards and each other.

"I'd like to know what in the hell happened here," Denny said.

"You sound like you're accusing me," she said.

"What'd you do? Leave something out that attracted them? Or what?"

"That's just crazy," she said. "Anyway, they didn't start showing up until you started hitting the girlie bars."

"Now that's really crazy," Denny said. "What's that have to do with anything?"

"We've both read D.H. Lawrence," she mimicked. "All I know is, *I* didn't dream these up."

"And I did, is that what you're saying? I dreamed them up? Pretty vivid dream, wouldn't you say. Real blood and all."

"As if I haven't been bleeding for the past five months and nine days. As if I ever stop bleeding." Through a red haze, she remembered Scottie head down in a red metal ice chest. She saw herself jogging to the park, late, working up a sweat to account for any smell on her body. She saw herself checking the diamond and then locating Denny in the outfield, dancing and hollering *mine, baby, mine,* and she saw the ball drop perfectly into his leather palm, and she saw him throw to second. She saw the scattered blankets and the picnic baskets and the children and the dogs. She saw Scottie hanging over the side of the red ice chest, past his center of gravity.

"You think I don't bleed?" Denny said. "He was for God's sake my child too. You've been accusing me for months now. Oh so polite, never a word. But you've been accusing me all along."

The wind changed direction and shot rain at the kitchen window across from them. Most of the rat snakes squirmed mildly on the floor, as if they were only tired litter now that they'd arranged for the man and the woman to light on the kitchen counter.

"You killed Scottie," she said. "There it is: you killed him. You let his little feet kick in the air for God knows how long, so busy pretending you're a high school star again that you don't even see your son head down in that ice water." Through the typhoon's wind, she remembered plucking Scottie out of the floating ice and beer cans.

"You weren't there," Denny said.

"I didn't need to be," she said. "You said you'd watch him until I got there."

"Where were you?" he said.

He leaned over the counter and pulled open the silverware drawer. He grabbed the steak knives and slammed the drawer shut as the snakes below the counter activated. "Where were you, Sheila?" he said. He aimed a steak knife at a dozing snake and struck him behind the head. The knife glanced off and the snake curled toward the storage room. "Where were you, Sheila?"

"You know where I was," she said.

"I guess I do," he said.

"I was jogging," she said. "Catching up at home and then jogging to meet you at the park. What is this?"

Denny aimed another steak knife. This time the knife stuck in the head, though the snake continued to writhe on the kitchen floor. She thought he looked more in ecstasy than in pain.

"I ain't so dumb, Sheila. I've got eyes. I've got ears. I've even got a nose, believe it or not. So who was the snake you were with when your son drowned?"

"Snake?" she said. "Is that a joke?"

"I don't think so," Denny said. He aimed the third steak knife at a third snake. "I wish this were a dirt floor," he said, "so I could skewer the bastards."

"Give me one," Sheila said. He handed her a steak knife and she threw. The knife skittered away on the tile floor.

"It was Brian Pemberton," she said.

"It was Brian?" he said. "Brian all along? Jesus. Jesus. What the hell for? Brian Pemberton couldn't have saved you from any damn thing."

"Not that you did either," she said. She picked up another knife. "Not that you have." This time the knife stuck, and the snake lay still.

Dennis picked up the remaining knives. "I can't stand this," he said. He stood on the counter. "Think of it: wife screws lover, husband makes perfect catch, son drowns in goddamn ice chest. I can't stand it." He hurled the handful of knives at the snakes on the floor and they bounced away harmlessly.

"There was a hole in me," she said. "I thought there was, anyway. I thought everything would leak away. I thought Brian would stop it up." At last she was weeping. "And now look: I'm as empty as . . . as . . . I don't know what."

"As me," he said.

But guilts do not cancel each other out, she thought. No.

Dennis and Sheila opened the other drawers beneath the overhanging counter and pulled out all the can openers, paring knives, corkscrews, forks, and carving knives. All night they aimed and flung utensils at the black rat snakes, killing dozens. *Ha!* they yelled. *Got the sucker!* Or—*Damn! Missed the bastard that time.* All night the typhoon surrounded them, whipping the tangantangan, blowing over the banana tree and ruining the tiny green fruit forever.

By three, the snakes were dead or comatose. The sea tossed incandescent foam upward, lighting the kitchen. Dennis walked carefully over the glossy tile, opened the cupboard above the stove, and brought out the whiskey. They remained on the countertop, trading slugs from the bottle. They did not make love yet, did not make a new child, there on the glossy black tile. There were no more knives to skewer any more snakes.

At dawn they walked out. The house was littered with dead or sleeping, sated rat snakes. Nothing struck at them. And they struck at nothing. Sheila felt herself slowly filling, as if her body were an hourglass. Dennis dried the distributor cap on the car and they drove to the airport.

There were no flights out because of the typhoon, and they sat together in the hot airport for seven hours. The company will pack our stuff, Dennis said. They'll ship it out. Sheila wondered if the moving crew would find the snakes they'd summoned. When the storm had spiraled hundreds of miles to the south, leaving only recalcitrant sputters of rain, they got on a flight to Japan. Eventually they would land in San Francisco, where they would not stay, having seen clearly both that northern light and the shimmering tropics. Dennis and Sheila buried their son at sea and spiraled together beyond guilt.

Home is the Hunter

"We're bringing her home this Friday, Lynette," Mother said. "So put sheets on her bed, will you?"

Nobody ever had to say her name. It was Charlotte. Nobody said it much. Just *she*, just *her*. She wouldn't answer to it, anyway. You had to call her Cherie, which Mother and Dad wouldn't do. I did sometimes, but it didn't matter. It might as well be *she*. The pronoun that needed no antecedent. Mrs. Ensfield in third period English would never believe that one, standing on the little platform she had her desk on so she could look down on us, giving us the word from above, saying you can't get the pronoun too far from the antecedent. Except in Charlotte's case. The pronoun case. The case of the lone pronoun. Except she was no pro-noun—she was a con-noun. Anything they wanted from her, she was against it. Then I thought of another meaning for *con* and pictured my sister's face behind the wrought-iron scrollwork at the window.

"Maybe the striped sheets," Mother said. "She might like those oranges and reds. Do you think? That might make her feel at home."

I'd never moved any of my things into her side of the room. There was nothing to clean. The sets of dog and horse books which had been suitable for us when we were children stood perfectly upright and tight, like slices of wheat bread, on the white shelf above my bed. Then the *Children's Illustrated Bible Stories* with plastic covers like on library books. It was like snooping on Joseph and his coat and Noah and his toy ark through dirty windows. They were all hers, too, but she didn't want them any more. Next the Lloyd C. Douglas novels they'd let me read, though they'd raised their eyebrows some. Then the pallid Christian stories I always got for presents, some crippled girl always ending up climbing a mountain for Jesus. Finally the gray-backed library books which I pretended were my own. *The Idiot. Billy Budd.* They figured those books were all right. Classics were all right.

I put the old Snoopy sheets on her bed. Orange and red stripes would just work her up. I put the pink bedspread back on her bed. I could say I thought we ought to save the good sheets for Grandma and Grandpa. But I set Smoochy, my favorite stuffed creature, over on her pillow. The rest of the family were all bunched up on my bed against the wall just staring across the canyon at Smoochy.

They'd been going to go get her on Friday but the floor mother from the home called Friday morning and said she was being grounded for trying to unscrew the bars from her window. We were sitting at the dinette table eating scrambled eggs mixed with rice. Yesterday it was scrambled eggs with grits. Today scrambled eggs with rice. Tomorrow scrambled eggs with grits. I wondered what Grandma thought.

"Do we still have the board?" Dad said. "Looks like I might need it."

"What'd she do?" I said.

"You just mind your eggs, Missy," Mother said.

"After dinner they're allowed to stroll around the grounds before dark," he said. All I could think of was belles in gowns over corsets, strolling in the evening cool as if they had wheels instead of feet. Cherie with such a bunch? "She just walked around the back to her window and unscrewed the bars from the concrete," Dad said. "They don't know how she came by the screwdriver."

He shook his head sorrowfully as if the collection basket had too much silver and not enough bills on the purple napkin. "That little gal is strong," he said.

They'd started with the board when we were thirteen. She'd been going out the window at night. Sometimes I woke up to see her blue-jeaned rear end on the sill just before she sprang into the weeds below. Once the police brought her home. She never would say what she'd been doing. One policeman said she was just walking toward town but it wasn't safe for a kid at this hour. I'd put my robe and slippers on and stood in the hallway to the living room.

You should have told us, Lynette, Mother said. *Why'd you just let her go like that? You want her to get hurt? Do you?*

Dad nailed the screen in, and when she just cut it with a kitchen knife and sprang out into the weeds again, he was waiting. First they tied her hands to the bedposts so she had to sleep on her back, which wasn't her sleeping position. *We hate to do this, Charlotte,* he told her. She'd just lain flat on her back with her lean face unmoving and her eyes closed. *It's what the church counselors said.* She never cried. I used to cry all the time, it seemed like. I still cried. One time I'd overheard Mother on the phone long distance to Grandma: *She's a dry-eyed one. She's a hard-hearted one. We finally had to take it to the church.*

Standing in the hallway in my robe and slippers, I'd watched the other policeman checking things out. Maybe she'd told. What did he see? The sleep-rumpled little family: mother, gray-haired father, correct daughter in pink bathrobe. The living room, vacuumed and dusted, the Olan Mills portrait on the whatnot shelf—Mother and me in pastels, Dad in some funeral suit, the other one in a red sweater, a wild grin on her face—the ripped chair cover and the stacks of newspapers in the corner, which my fastidious mother somehow lived with. That policeman looked puzzled. Why had he brought the outsider into this house?

The board: it was a raw pine two-by-four plank. The ones in the shed had nails, so he'd bought the board new from Spangler's lumber yard: Yeah, Jack, I just need me a clean plank to whop my girl, she broke the hairbrush that used to be my implement. Can't tie that filly down, gotta do something, and the folks at the Baptist said a board'd be the thing.

After the first time, she'd taken the board from the shed and hidden it somewhere or thrown it away somehow. She never said she did. He visited Spangler's again. After the next time, she painted a cartoon on the board with magic markers and nail polish which she kept hidden in the weeds below our window. It showed a tall, cavernous, gray-haired man with the board upraised over his head, with the girl crouched beneath—with her tongue stuck out. The tongue was done in Hot Pink Glossy nail polish. On the picture of the upraised board was another tiny cartoon of the gray-haired man and the crouching girl, tongue and all. He used the board anyway. I wondered if he held it picture up or picture down.

"We'll just have to take Grandma and Grandpa over to get her on Sunday then," Dad said. "Won't hurt to let them see her there anyway. Maybe they'll start to understand."

"I thought I told you to put the good sheets on her bed, Missy," Mother said.

"I know, but I thought we ought to save them for Grandma," I said.

"Well, that was nice," she said. Oh, wasn't I nice. "But—I don't know—they're kind of bright. And Grandma. . . ."

"Grandma loves bright things," I said. "They're *her*!"

I'd always known they weren't my real grandparents, even before anybody told me. They couldn't have been my mother's parents. Grandma cooked things in a wok, she wore orange and red clothes that would match the sheets, she sent me T-shirts for my birthdays and once a red canvas purse. I knew she'd take me shopping and I could get that cotton sweater, and they couldn't say anything if she bought it for me. We'd whirl through the mall stores and stop finally and have sundaes. I wouldn't even care if Charlotte had to come along. We were more sisters when Grandma took us out than we ever were in the room together. When my mother shopped, she took five hours to pick out the perfect dishcloth. Grandma was Mother's aunt. Mother's parents had died when she was eighteen, and it was too late for Grandma to work on her. And then she married Dad, of course.

"Those sheets," Mom said. "I don't know." She looked at Dad, but he was pressing the tines of his fork onto the last bits of egg-and-rice on his plate. "You're old enough," Mom said. "You ought to know. Your grandma's not going to be with us much longer. The Lord wants your grandma at His side."

Mother smiled at the thought, shaking her head: Grandma right up there with the celebrity. "Now, He'll tell her in His own time," she said. "You're not to mention it, you hear?"

"You hear, Missy?" Dad said.

All that day I sat through classes and gradually I forgot that she was dying. I was supposed to forget, anyway. I wasn't supposed to tell. Everybody knew she was dying except Grandma. By the time

I'd finished fifth period P.E. and got out of my gym suit and back into my clothes and made it to geometry, I didn't believe she was dying. She didn't know it, so how could she die? I did my proofs and forgot that she wasn't going to be with us much longer.

That night Grandma died in my sleep. Someone was beating her with Charlotte's board, and I could see the little girl with her bright pink tongue protruding, but I didn't know who was wielding it. I woke before dawn with the bedspread on the floor and the top sheet twisted around my legs. I got up and crept down the hall to the linen closet and got out the other old set of Snoopy sheets and remade my bed, just as if I'd wet the bed. Charlotte wouldn't think that I was trying to be the superior sister if I had those old kiddie sheets on my bed, too.

Grandma and Grandpa pulled up in their camper before supper on Saturday. They both hugged me just as if they, not the Lord, loved me. She was wearing blue jeans and a red and blue plaid shirt. Her camping clothes, she said. There was no death on her anywhere, not on my grandma.

On Sunday after church we all drove over to get Charlotte. We took the station wagon, which meant one of us would have to crouch in the back all the way home. I thought it should be her, not me. Mom went in to get her and the rest of us waited in the car.

"Suppose you all can wait for dinner?" Dad said. "I know Momma's got the chicken ready to fry up."

I was starving. While Mother and Dad had gone to Bible Study before service, Grandma had made French toast, and I'd stuffed myself. Egg bread, Grandpa had called it. But that was hours ago.

Grandpa said he wanted to take us out for Sunday dinner if there was someplace on the way back.

Dad said she wasn't supposed to have any treats.

"But these are exceptional times," Grandpa said. I saw him look straight at Dad. I knew he meant *she's dying*. Grandma hadn't been looking but she squeezed my shoulder and asked me where I wanted to go shopping. Suddenly I was afraid to go shopping with her: I might say *Grandma, you can't die*.

Then Mother was standing at Dad's window. "She can't come," she said.

"She can't come?" Dad said. "Is that what they say? Who's paying for this, anyway? Of course she's coming."

"Well, she's done something else," Mother said. "So they can't let her leave."

"Done something? Now she's done something?" Dad looked desperately around. He'd left his board at home. He opened the car door and unfolded himself in the hot air outside.

Then I was alone with them, Grandpa who knew, and Grandma who wouldn't be with us much longer but didn't know it. She would leave her body and she would go to the Lord and she would have eternal life. Dad said.

"It's not easy, is it, Lynette?" she said.

What? What?

"You know we love Charlotte, too." She smiled. "For years when she was that spunky chub I wanted to take her home."

Grandpa shook his head at her.

"Oh, don't shush me, Al. She lives here, after all."

Doesn't she. She lives with her classics hanging above her, laid out on her faded Snoopy sheets, surrounded by all her stuffed family.

"They just never were the right folks for her, that's all," Grandma said.

Then we watched them coming down the walk. Mother and Dad had her by the elbows, grimly. She was walking fast, making them take extra little steps, walking tight into herself as if their hands were not on her elbows. A man walking ahead of them unlocked the gate, let them through, and stayed close while Dad opened the back of the station wagon and pointed her in. Fetch! I wanted to say. Beg! Play dead!

Grandma leaned over the back seat and tried to give her a hug. She endured it. Grandma chatted to her cheerfully, saying she wanted to take us shopping and we could pick out our birthday presents early.

Maybe she'd heard the Lord whispering to her after all, I thought.

Charlotte wouldn't say a thing. I said, "What'd you do to make them ground you?" She wouldn't even look at me. Behind us the dust of the long road to the Home sprayed out, and then we turned onto the highway. Bent over in the back, she suddenly began singing. "I wanna know where love is," she belted out. We weren't allowed rock music.

"None of that," Dad said.

"I wanna go where love is," she sang, but more quietly. She hummed all the way through Taylorsville, even when Grandma said, "Is that a Boy George tune, Charlotte?" I couldn't even answer for her, though I knew it wasn't any Boy George. "Those aren't bad lyrics," Grandma said softly, not commenting on their morality but conceding some poetic value.

Just past Taylorsville, Dad stopped at Mom and Pop's Log Cabin. Red checkered curtains at a picture window framed a sign: Home-cooked Dinners Served Family Style.

"Now, Dad, what about—" Mother said.

"Hush," he said. "I know you've got those birds ready. They're not going to get up and fly away, are they?" He laughed. "Grandpa wants to take us out for Sunday dinner."

As he helped Mother out of the back seat, he said, low, "I *know* what they said. But I guess I can do what I want with her, can't I? She's mine, bought and paid for, and I'm the one paying them."

The restaurant had a fake log front, the logs thickly shellacked. Grandpa lined us up and took our pictures, first all of us, then Grandma and the two of us. "Now just you girls," he said. Charlotte giggled and began striking poses. "Hey, that's the way," Grandpa said, and began clicking away. Charlotte stuck her chest out, put one hand behind her neck and the other on her hip, and made a kissy mouth. Mother laughed in embarrassment. I stepped away, and Charlotte posed, flinging her hair up with both hands, turning and looking back over her shoulder. A family walking out of Mom and Pop's Log Cabin stared and I heard the mother whisper, "Model."

Inside we sat at a long wooden table with a red-checkered tablecloth. A waitress in a red-checkered apron over a long pioneer-woman dress handed out menus and began setting silverware and plates before us.

"I guess family style means the patriarch orders," Grandpa said. He began pointing out dishes on the menu to the waitress.

"I want lobster," Charlotte said.

"Now, this is Grandpa's treat," Mother told her. "He's the one ordering for all of us."

"How come I always have to do what everybody else does?" Charlotte said. "'Family Style,'" she said bitterly. "That means they hold you down and force-feed you until you look like their little dumpling. Well, I'm having lobster."

Suddenly Charlotte the flamboyant model looked like the little girl strapped into a high chair, long legs dangling below the foot rest. How long had it gone on? I could remember sitting on the kitchen floor until the backs of my legs were dented in the pattern of the linoleum. They wouldn't let her eat and they wouldn't let her eat, and I'd sit crying softly, though she wouldn't cry even then. Finally they held out a bowl of mashed potatoes, and Dad spooned it into her. She spit it back at him. He'd spoon a mound in and hold her mouth closed with one hand, put down the bowl and spoon, and stroke her throat with the other hand until she swallowed. Again and again and again. I could see Mom behind the high chair, one hand fisted and the other holding the fist just below her chin, crying until Charlotte threw up and then unbuckling her from the high chair and carrying her into the bathroom.

Grandma put her arm across Charlotte's back. "Look, honey, they don't have lobster on the menu."

I watched her settle beneath Grandma's arm and then shudder.

"You girls better go wash up," Dad said. I pushed back my chair obediently. Charlotte said, "Je-sus," and pulled away from Grandma's arm.

In the bathroom, we each took a stall and from inside the gray box, I said, "What'd you do this time?"

She giggled. "You should see what it says in here," she said. "Anybody write anything in yours?"

"Really," I said. "What'd you do?"

"What is this, a confession booth or something?" she said. "Forgive me, sister, for I have sinned." There was a flush. I imagined her sins swirling around and sucked down into the public toilet. "All's I did was start up a food fight. Jesus H. Christ, you shoulda seen it. I launch me a sausage and it thwops right into MaryBeth Peters's cheek, and she grabs a fistful of scrambled eggs and heaves 'em back, and then there's breakfast every which way."

She giggled. "And there's that slob Donna Curtain stuffing her face as fast as she can, intercepting sausages and toast and whonking 'em down."

Her head appeared beneath the stalls' partition. "Hey," she said, "hurry it up. I wanna see what it says in there."

"*Char*-lotte," I said, "leave me alone." I pulled my skirt down over my knees.

"'Leave me alone,'" she mimicked. "Isn't that what I try to do, Miss Holy Priss?"

At the sink, I saw our two unsisterly faces in the mirrors. I could see Mom and Dad's little genes bumping along in the blood beneath the skin of my round face. "Why'd you do it?"

"Say 'Cherie.' Say, 'Why'd you do it, Cherie oh lovely one?'"

"Cherie," I said to the towel dispenser.

"You don't know?" she said. "You mean you really don't know?"

At the table, Dad said, "We were about ready to come and fish you two out."

"Well, you know how it is with sisters," Mother said. "Sisters must have a lot to catch up on." She laughed in her mild, cover-up way.

The food was coming in big bowls set in the middle of the long table. There was chicken and ham and mashed potatoes and gravy and wax beans and biscuits and I don't know what all.

"Hey, watch the way you're passing," Grandpa said. "You know what it means if those dishes cross each other."

He always said that. It meant someone would get married soon.

"Nobody eligible here," Dad said. "And besides, I haven't met the man brave enough to take on Charlotte."

You, I thought: the brave man with the cartoon board.

I made a crater in my potatoes for the gravy. I watched Grandma's arm go over Charlotte's shoulder again. I started forking in my mashed potatoes, neatly, dutifully, their blood and muscles in me moving my right hand with the fork to my mouth. It was always Charlotte, Charlotte, wherever she was, however good I was.

"No, it'll take a wrestler to wrangle that girl down," Dad said.

Grandma patted Charlotte's shoulder. "Ease up, Walt," she said. "Be glad you've got her home again."

Home is the Hunter

Dad looked chastened at his ham. Once when we were at Grandma and Grandpa's, he was trying to spank Charlotte in the yellow bedroom upstairs. I'd been sitting on the orange and yellow bedspread reading and trying not to watch him grab her and then lose her, swat at her and command her—*No daughter of mine would do that*—to submit and repent. I was crying and Charlotte was leaping over the other bed away from him. Then downstairs Grandma started banging out "Rock of Ages" on her piano, and Dad collapsed beside the bed with that chastened look. I thought he was going to cry or pray, and Charlotte and I ran downstairs.

"We *are* glad to have you home, dear," Mother said. She peered across the table out of her round face. Grandma was just patting away. Charlotte was home again.

"Home is the sailor, home from the sea," I said suddenly. "And Cherie, home from the Home."

At Grandma's look, I'd instantly remembered why the sailor was home from the sea, the hunter home from the hill. They were dead.

Charlotte twisted away from Grandma's arm. "You don't always have to be de*fend*ing me," she said. "I can take care of myself."

"Charlotte!" Mother said. "Be nice to your grandma."

She shoved in a spoonful of mashed potatoes. "Why the hell?" she said through the potatoes. "Why the hell be nice? Everybody always wants me to *be nice*. She comes to see me once a year." She tried to swallow the potatoes and gagged. "Sends me a few letters and stupid cutesy-cute cards and some nightshirt or something. And thinks she's my *grand*mother."

At last Charlotte was crying. She spit the last of the mashed potatoes into her napkin. "She's no grandmother of mine," she said. She didn't know how to cry, I thought. She was bucking in the chair as if she was about to throw up.

The waitress was at the table with a man wearing a red-checkered vest. "Please," he said. "What's the problem, folks? We can't have all this here."

"Scram," Grandma told him. Then she pulled Charlotte to her and held her.

Charlotte was crying against Grandma, melting against her, shrinking into the adopted sister who was no daughter of theirs like

I was, shrinking into some little girl who wouldn't be able to take the board uncrying any more. At night beneath my stories, surrounded by my stuffed family, I pretended Grandma was my mother really and I was the adopted one and soon she'd come and take me and explain why she'd left me with them all these lost years. My grandmother and my Cherie were melting together.

I got up and tried to pull them apart from behind. "Listen, Cherie," I said. "Get away from her. She's dying anyway."

They did pull apart. They looked at me, Charlotte's face blotchy red, Grandma's face yellow-gray above her red jacket.

"—ask you to leave," the man was saying.

Dad was up and coming for me. I started out, past the long tables of Sunday families staring with red-checkered tablecloths reflected in their nice faces, wanting him to follow me and take the board to me in the parking lot.

All the way back, we bumped around in the station wagon trying not to touch. There was nothing to say. Once Mother said, "There's where the new Kmart's going up." At the house everyone separated. Grandma and Grandpa went for a drive in their self-contained van.

At last at night, untucked-in between our faded Snoopy sheets, we waited. She'd left Smoochy beside her pillow. She could have it, I thought, and the whole stuffed family. I thought we should switch now, and I should be driven away, crouching in the rear of the station wagon.

At last Grandma was in our room. She wore a long blue robe. She set my white desk chair between our beds and reached one hand out to each of us.

"You look like an angel, Grandma," Charlotte said.

And she did, floating in the dark on the glowing white chair, the sleeves of her blue robe spread out like wings.

"I already knew," she said. "I hate it. I can't stand it. But I already knew."

She was squeezing my shoulder and I knew her other hand was squeezing Charlotte.

"I'm so sorry I couldn't be your mother," she said. "But then I'm sorry for plenty. Like never sleeping in a tent in the summer with your grandpa again."

Home is the Hunter

I saw her sleek burnished box slid lengthwise into her slot at the mausoleum. I fell asleep with her hand on my back, my breath sending out into the common air, my lungs sucking up the world with her forever in it.